BLACK KRIM
a novel

KATE WYER

COBALT PRESS
Baltimore, MD

Cobalt Press
Baltimore, MD

cobaltreview.com/cobalt-press

For all inquiries, including requests for review materials, please contact cobalt@cobaltreview.com.

For Mom and Dad

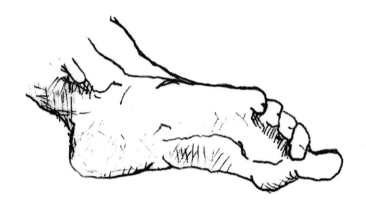

BLACK KRIM

From my window I watch the old man turn circles in the field. There is snow, not much, but enough to cover the ground. He is barefoot and walking with his head down, a single dark figure against the declining light.

I let the curtain fall back against the sill and move toward the phone, but instead of calling anyone, I return to the window again. The man is still circling. I pull on my gloves, my coat, my boots and now move toward him without hesitation.

He looks up at me and stops walking. The cold shakes him.

"Come with me," I say. I offer my gloved hand. He reaches for it, takes it. He is silent. He trips a little, his feet red and stiff, the bones bold struts.

"Keep your head down, out of the wind," I tell him, and I rub his large hand between my small ones. He smiles in a childish way. He listens, ducks into the wind and shelters his face. His large ears are red, his lips blue. His balding scalp shines.

We cross the field, the street, the front yard. The dogs jump at him as he crosses the threshold.

"Get down, Macie!" he says and pulls his arms up into his body, away from the excited animals. His voice is louder than I expected.

"That's Blue and that's Wilson," I say and look into his face.

"I don't have a Macie."

The old man laughs. He stands in the doorway looking down at his feet. The dogs lick the water pooling on the floor from his wet hems. They take big snorting breaths of him and then, tails still wagging, leave the room. I give him a large towel and he wipes his face and head, dries his hands and then drops it to the floor. He uses his left foot to cover the right with the towel, rubs it dry, then shifts feet and dries the other the same way. He looks up at me, waiting.

"Come sit down." I gesture toward the kitchen. He leaves the towel on the floor, follows me. The old man pulls out a chair at the table and sits down, places his hands on the tablecloth, palms up. He stares at the redness of his fingers. A thin clear light catches in the fluid collecting in the rim of his nostril. His face confirms what I thought from the window. He doesn't know where he is, what he was doing out there.

"What's your name?" I ask and lean into the doorframe.

He wipes his nose with his sleeve, but he doesn't respond.

"Where do you live?" I try.

He looks like a child who knows violence, who knows how to avoid it. He shrugs, a slight lifting of the shoulders, and then rubs his palms together. They make a dry scraping sound, like when a window opens after a long cold spell.

I put water on for coffee and then leave to see what clothing I have to fit him; the strangeness of the situation starting to become more real, now that the immediate danger from the cold is over. I dig through my old dresser, pause to push the hair out of my face and then pull it back into a ponytail. Sweatpants, old and with busted elastic, will have to do. I drape them over my neck and then run water in the tub until it becomes warm. There is a dried out palm tree in a blue ceramic pot in the corner of the bathroom. It came with the house, with the previous owner's lack of attention. The pot looks big enough to hold the man's feet, bigger than any bowl I have. I tip it over, grab the trunk of the tree, thump it out of the container and leave it all—the dirt, the root ball, the plant—on the tile. I fill the pot with water a few times, swirling out the remaining dirt, and then carry it downstairs.

The old man startles when I return.

I put the pot on the floor. "I got you these," I say and hand him the pants.

He stands, loosens his belt and drops his jeans. I turn my back to him quickly, surprised.

He taps me on the shoulder to tell me that he's finished changing and then hands me his wet jeans. The sweatpants are tight on him and come to about mid-calf. He does a half-squat to try to stretch them a little and then sits back in the chair, eases his feet into the warm water.

I feel the jean pockets for a wallet and don't find one.

"You lost your wallet?"

"No, I don't believe so."

"It's not in your pants. Is it in your shirt pocket?"

He feels the front pockets of his flannel and shakes his head.

"You musta taken it already." He doesn't seem concerned.

My hair is wet at the temples from the snow, my nerves, and the effort to bring the man in from the cold. I rub my sleeve against my head to dry the dampness and then throw his pants down the stairs to the basement, to put them in the dryer after he's settled.

I start to respond, then stop. The coffee pot finishes its cycle; it hisses and bubbles the last of the water.

"You should have something warm to drink."

The man shakes his head no, reconsiders, then nods yes. I pour two cups and place one in front of him.

"I have milk, not cream. Do you want some? And brown sugar—that's the only kind I have."

"Yes, that's fine with me." I add the milk and brown sugar, place a spoon into the mug.

"Who can I call to come get you?"

He moves his feet in the bowl, shifts them slightly. A small wave passes over the lip onto the floor. The dogs come back into the room and then settle near my feet as I stand at the counter.

I should call the cops, I think. He has slumped a little, his coloring closer to healthy. The warmth of the water and the room are making him sleepy. I've never known an elderly man. No grandfathers, no father. No uncles, no older brothers. I study his long eyebrows, his white stubble, and the lines around his mouth.

He is still silent. *Does he even have anyone to call? What if he doesn't—if he's homeless?*

I walk up the stairs to the spare bedroom. I've never changed the sheets., never needed to. The room is one I imagined filling when I bought the house. I imagined company. I turn around in the room, seeing it again, looking at it with a stranger's eyes. A mirror and a dresser from a yard sale. A framed print of some feathers blowing down the beach. Striped wallpaper in light grays and blues. A few clumps of dog hair by the baseboards. I turn on the bedside lamp.

He'll be more together after some sleep.

I call to him from the top of the stairs. "You should lie down. I have the guest room ready."

I hear him remove his feet from the bowl and then the grunt as he walks back to the hallway to get the towel he left there. The dogs' chains shake as they too get up. He stands at the foot of the stairs, puts his hand on the railing.

"Thank you," he says and concentrates on the steps. I wait for him at the top and then move aside to push the door open a little more. He nods, closes the door behind him. The bed takes his weight and the light clicks out. I stand there a moment longer in the dark hallway, hear his strange breaths.

My head becomes raw as the heat leaves. The heat leaves me through my head, my feet. The darkness of a snow-sky, a white-lie, and more snow coming. Black corn stalks sharp against my instep. I count my steps in the circle. I am waiting for her to see me. I know she will. Movement in the corner of my sight. Again, around again. My head raw. She would have come if I had shoes on. A circle worn in the snow, blood cooling in my toes; shoes by the side of the road, the socks neatly tucked inside. Across the field. She is coming across the field.

I wake to the sounds of the dogs coming in from outside. I smell coffee. I throw on my robe in a panic, push my feet into beat-up slippers and clomp down the stairs. I stop at the last step, wait to see what's going on. My guest has made himself breakfast—eggs and toast.

"Macie and the other one had to go out," he says. He takes a forkful of egg, puts it on a bite of toast and then eats.

I tie my robe tighter and cross my arms in front of my chest. I clear the sleep from my throat.

"Blue, Wilson," I point. "Did you feed them?"

"No, just myself." He smiles. "I wasn't sure how late you were going to sleep."

I look at the clock—it's only 6:00 in the morning. It's Saturday.

"Do you know where you are? Who I am?" I ask, not leaving the step. I pull my hair into a ponytail, smooth its knots. The two dogs are begging the man for his food.

"I didn't sleep very well. I needed to eat."

His feet look cold and dry. The house is set at 60 degrees, not warm enough for an old man.

I move off the step and toward the pantry. I grab two handfuls of dry dog food and fill their bowls. They push in and eat.

"They're good dogs," he says.

I sit across the table from him, feel the absurdity of my decision to let him spend the night, feel the strangeness of sharing the room with him in this familiar way. The absurdity of this man making himself breakfast in my house. He stands, gets me a mug from the cabinet and pours me some coffee. I nod thanks and wrap my hands around it. We sit together this way, not moving, until I lift the cup to drink.

"I remember you like black coffee," he says.

"What else do you remember from yesterday? How are you feeling?"

"I'm stiff," he says, moves his ankles in circles. He squeezes his hands into fists and then releases them, repeats the motion.

"You have my pants? I'd like them back." He looks at me with clear eyes, with an awareness that was absent last night.

"Sure," I say and push back from the table. "Once they're dry, I'll call somebody for you." I walk to the basement and put his pants in the dryer, turn it on. I turn my neck to try to crack it. The muscles are tight with nerves. I talk myself down a little, *He's still confused—making himself breakfast like he's home?*

I walk back up from the basement. His back is to me. He has long arms and thin muscles. His ears stand parallel to his head, something his age accentuated—ears get a little longer each year, the cells unable to turn off like other body cells. I think of my grandmother and her ears, her nose, and how the photos over the years show those two features growing in prominence. It seems like a plan to have the elderly resemble each other, to look less like the familiar person you grew up with: biology creates distance.

He turns his torso my way, aware that I'm watching him.

"It'll just be ten minutes or so until they're dry," I say. I begin to make my own breakfast. I pull out the cutting board and chop green onions for an omelet. I choose a few mushrooms. He reclines in the chair, stretches his long legs out and under the table, stretches his arms above his head. I whisk eggs together and pour them into the pan, add the onions and mushrooms. The omelet turns a pale brown. Anxiety returns to my neck and shoulder muscles. I eat standing at the counter, add some salt, some pepper.

The dryer buzzes as I finish. I put the plate in the sink and go collect the pants.

Thank you," he says and stands. He pulls down the borrowed sweatpants. I turn my head again, instinctively. I hear him shake out the jeans before slipping them on. His lack of embarrassment, or maybe lack of awareness, is alarming. He hasn't noticed my reactions to his near nakedness. There was a strange intimacy in his audacity—an assumed familiarity almost. As if I had been around for years and no longer counted as a stranger, as a woman. It brought attention to my prudishness, though. I blushed so intensely it hurt my cheeks.

I hear the kitchen chair scrape backwards and turn around. He has settled back into his place at the table and folded my pants over the back of the chair.

"Who can I call to tell you're okay? Someone must be worried?" I let the question hang.

"I don't have anyone to call."

"Where do you live?"

"I don't have a house, not anymore."

I clear my throat

"You're homeless?"

He doesn't answer, but shame fills his quiet face.

"What were you doing last night, in the snow? Where are your shoes?"

He hunches his shoulders up again, again looking like a child.

"I don't know. I'm not sure."

How have I helped him? I wonder. The choice to let him stay would be a hard one to explain to my mom, to the police.

"Okay. I'm going to get dressed. Then we can see if there's somewhere you can go. Take it from there."

He focuses on the table and the movement of his hands around the square pattern of the cloth.

I click the light out, pull the blanket up to my nose, cover it, and attempt to cover my ears. I tuck the edge of it against the back of my neck to keep out the cold. The warm water in the planter helped—dark particles of potting soil floating, feet turning pink, the toes last and pricking—but the chill remains. It has settled into the damp weight of my body in her guest bed.

I want to sleep. I want to halt the planning and building of a new life. I hear her turning in the bed in the next room.

I feel shame.

As a child, my Corbina always wanted to know about her name. How did I choose it? How did I know Corbina was the right name for her? She couldn't understand the business of taking a guess or picking something pretty. She wanted oracles, divination. She wanted to be sure she had been given the right name.

I told her, when she was eight—maybe, no, maybe nine or ten, the story of her grandfather surf fishing the day I was born. My mother wasn't, isn't, a woman to ask for anything. She hadn't asked him to be there, at the birth, so he didn't go. It might not have occurred to him to be there. He had passions after all, and parenting wasn't one of them.

Her name, Corbina, is a type of saltwater fish. My father, before he left, told me how corbinas ride the breakers into the shallows to root out sand crabs. The fish are exposed, their backs out of the water, their tough snouts in the sand. He described lunging at them with nets.

When the story was over, she nodded and accepted this splinter. She understood it would eventually be absorbed or work its way out of her body. I was surprised she understood. She connected her name with my father's parental reluctance, her own father's absence and my bitterness. I saw it in the dark cast of her eyes. I had hoped she would be distracted by the stories of the beach. I had prepared other stories, lies, I guess—lies that would have been kinder in some ways—but, when she asked, I told her the truth in the clearest way I could.

Corbina told people her name was a variation of Corinna, a name that meant girl.

"I get to pick now," she told me after her teacher called one afternoon to report the change.

"I pick Corinna, as in girl, not fish."

"Corbina is so pretty. And no one has it, anywhere—probably."

"Exactly."

She was Corinna for several grades, all the way up through middle school and her first year of high school. She switched back to Corbina sophomore year, without ceremony or explanation. I was convinced it had something to do with angst, with not knowing who she was at that age. If she didn't feel like a girl, like a person, she might as well be a fish. I didn't ask. It was up to her.

The morning starts well enough. The room is freezing. I see she has closed the heating vent, most likely to save on her bill, the room unused. Up, a quiet walk down the stairs, a familiarness in the stock of her pantry, the layout of her dishes. Everything here chosen for comfort. The dogs swirl around my feet, their thick tails making a mass of white as they circle, tongues out and eyes begging. I lean back in a chair at the kitchen table.

"Ben," I say out loud.

Does the mind change when the name does?

"Steven." No.

I feel a shock of pleasure in choosing my own name. I let the dogs outside. They streak through the doorway, pushing themselves forward, propelled by distant instincts, perpetual puppies; domesticated brains shrunken by comfort.

I call to the dogs and have them climb the steps with me to my bedroom. I lock us inside. They jump onto the bed and curl into each other, their eyes on me. We all seem to be listening for movement. Most of me hopes he just leaves. I hope for the sound of the door opening and then closing, the quiet of my house returning. I know this won't happen. He won't leave without a coat, without shoes. But, whatever gap was formed last night, whatever loss or trauma, isn't present in this morning.

But there is an opposite want, too. The want to be startled into conflict, to have an upset in my daily routines and operations. My mind turns against this upset, thinks of physical risks, judges the weight and heft of objects, selects a paperweight, and makes it new with this consideration.

He's old, a visitor who spent the night in my house, a man whom I let sleep in the bedroom next to mine and now seems less frail, less vulnerable. The paperweight is smooth and cool in my palm.

What would I do with this? I ask myself. I put it back on the dresser. The dogs have closed their eyes and are sleeping in the warmth of the sun. I get dressed in my grass-stained jeans, a man's button down shirt and a sweater. I put on fresh socks and step into my slippers. I realize I should turn the heat up.

I open the door; the man is at the top of the stairs.

"I'll go, if that's what you want, but I'd like to stay a little while. I don't have anywhere else to go. I have money." His eyes are soft, begging for respect, and the dignity of a place to stay.

My eyes move from his face to the doorknob, to the dogs and back. He watches my instant assessment. I close the door to him, slowly, and then sit on the bed next to Blue.

"What now?" I ask into a pink ear.

"My name is Martin," he says through the door. I hear the man move into the guest room and sit on the bed.

I reach for the cordless phone next to the bed and push 4. It autodials my mom. The phone rings, rings again and then I hang up. If she is home, she'll call me back. If not, then I don't have to tell her about Martin. I realize I'm not ready to have another person's influence on my decision.

I leave the room, move quickly down the stairs and grab my jacket from the front hallway before leaving the house. Outside, the cold pulls at my cheeks.

The greenhouse sits low next to the shed. It's dug down into the earth for warmth. Insulated windows frame the sides. The roof is corrugated metal with a small turbine turning in the wind. The door sticks a little as I push into the slightly warmer air inside. There are the remains of squash plants, their vines dried out, yellow, tough, and prickly. I need the space of the windowed room, the packed dirt floor, and the seedling trays. I need a place to think. I move to the dirt floor and hold my knees tight against my chest for warmth.

There is some part of me that enjoys this tension, that enjoys the intrusion of his company. It's a private thrill in my quiet life. It's a rush that accompanies an action whose outcome cannot be known.

Low clouds track over the flatness of the tidal basin. I see where a groundhog pushed aside the bricks and entered through a tunnel near the floor. There is nothing in here for them, not this time of year. I replace what dirt I can and stack the bricks back, knowing it is a useless gesture. I'll have to buy fox urine in the spring. How do they collect it? A fox farm with trays under cages? A factory to bottle it?

The man, Martin, hasn't asked me my name. He hasn't asked me anything about myself, like if anyone else lives at the house. There has been no discussion at all, and he wants to stay with me? I stare at the cold covered ground and my footprints leading here. The glass is starting to fog up a little. It creates a pale filter of breath and body heat. There has been a silence about all the average details. I just learned his name—a name last night I was sure he didn't remember. What else was there and not there? He has the childish mind of someone forgetting themselves; his memories eaten away by something not fully understood.

I stand and brush off the seat of my pants, brush my palms together to shake free any dirt. I step back into the wind and latch the greenhouse door behind me. My footprints crush dark marks back to the house.

Martin is still upstairs. I kick off my boots and hang up my jacket. I push up the sleeves of my sweater and start on the dishes. The warm water feels good on my hands. The plates stack up on the drying rack. The phone rings—my Mom.

"Hi," I say and dry my hands on a dish towel, cupping the phone between my chin and shoulder as I do.

"Hi," she says. "What are you doing later? Do you want to come over for dinner?"

I pause for too long and she senses I am making up a reason for why I can't.

"If you have plans, don't worry about it—just thought I'd ask." There is an awkward pulling back in her voice.

"No, no—I don't have plans. I was just thinking. Maybe lunch tomorrow would be better, though. I have some stuff to do around here. To clean up." I look around my kitchen and imagine my mom in her kitchen—a red lip stain, contoured cheekbones.

"Oh, yes. Whatever works for you," she says, stressed. We are not good at telling each other the truth. Both of us silent on the phone, waiting for the other to continue.

"My week's been okay," I say to finally break the quiet, "how was yours?"

"Okay, too. Busy." She doesn't offer the details of what busy is, but it's easy to imagine. She is part of some committees—the neighborhood group and another one, I can't remember what. Anything to keep her out of her own head.

"I was wondering," I start, picking the words carefully, "have you seen anything in the papers or on the news about a missing man?"

"A missing man? Missing how? What do you mean?"

"A lost person. Anyone searching for an old man—anything?"

"No, I haven't heard anything. What did you hear?"

"A neighbor mentioned something about it to me, asked if I knew anything. I said no, just thought I'd ask."

"I can check the 'vulnerable persons' bulletins at work. What else did he say?"

"We talked about how hard it would be to find someone if they were lost out in the fields."

"I'll ask around, see if he is anyone's case."

Shit, I think. "Thanks," I say.

"Call me tomorrow if your plans change, otherwise I'll come over tomorrow—okay? Around two?"

"That sounds good."

I replace the phone in its cradle and look toward the stairs. The small deception feels good. I have a secret. Now I have to figure out how to move around with it, carry the risk, the open question.

"Let me teach you how to cook," I'd say.

"No," she'd say. "I'm not interested in cooking."

"Cards, then. I'll teach you cards like your grandma taught me."

"No."

She looks at me with her dark eyes. An eleven year old.

"Why don't you want to do anything I want to teach you?"

"Because we aren't alike. I don't like those things."

"What do you like?"

"Eggs."

"How can you like eggs? How do you like eggs?"

She doesn't answer, just sort of tilts her head to the side. She takes a *National Geographic* and sits on the couch, near me. She searches for the page she left off. I, in turn, take up a book and flip it open to my cardboard bookmark. I watch her; she has found her place and is settling into the article. Her face relaxes. I feel my own shoulders drop some but I can't focus on the book. I just want to watch her, watch her process words and form pictures. She's doing it without me, somehow.

She feels my eyes on her and looks up. I look down to my page.

"You were watching me."

"Sure, I was."

I don't look up from the book, but I see her move so her back faces me. Once she's settled she starts to read again. I try to find the book more interesting than her. I fail, again, but in a more subtle way. I day-dream about her, about her future. I wonder if she'll have her own children, if I'll be a good grandmother. A better grandmother than a mother, I think, yes. Distance forms different bonds.

Later, Corbina's head starts to nod toward her chest. She wakes herself and then nods again. I reach for her magazine and then slide her feet up onto the couch. I pull a blanket over her and crouch beside her. I run my finger over her face, tracing the shapes. I follow her eyebrows, full like her father's, her nose, mine, the space between her nose and lips—her own. I trace her ears, like her grandmother's small shells, her cheekbones, like mine. She smiles sleepily.

I don't know what sort of genetics to expect from her body. I don't know what genes will turn on, what pathologies will ignite, what nature versus my nurturing will do. Her father's side is mostly unknown.

She hugs me as I stop tracing her face. It's a tight hug, a little aggressive even. She told me once that it was to shake the sadness from me, to squeeze it from me. It hasn't worked but she hasn't stopped squeezing. I am always surprised, each time she does it, by her willingness to hug. I have grown into them. My mother has one breast, a survivor. She never wanted anyone to know the falseness of her chest; she never pulled me in. How easy it is to explain each behavior—a science! A science. But how impossible to understand my daughter.

How could I tell her that my mind did not choose her father but my body did? What would I say?

I became accustomed to catching glimpses of people in self-conscious moments: the run to the mailbox in a towel, the bathrobe or pajamas; the person perched by the window waiting for a letter, cracking their knuckles and rubbing their palms on their thighs. Being a mailman was good for this reason, for the way people were between work selves and home selves; people caught in transition.

Corbina caught me off guard. She appeared in the window of an old farm house and I recognized her from the farmer's market. This was only the second time I had seen her, one of my last days at work. I was holding her phone bill and several mailers. I was also holding her name. Corbina. A name that surprised me with its roundness. A tall stone of a woman, a strong jaw with large teeth she probably ground in her sleep. The first time I saw her she was selling Black Krim heirlooms—giant ugly tomatoes that split their own seams. She was concentrating on a book about soil pH, barely registering anyone around her. She had kicked off her shoes and pushed her toes into the ground, digging them in, wriggle by wriggle, impatient to absorb what she needed to know. I took a dark purple tomato and kept walking. I didn't look back until I was in my truck. She hadn't noticed, her eyebrows still gathered, lips in a slight frown. I bit into the blackness. Juice ran down my chin.

Retirement came, a party with cake and blue icing, soda. We celebrate like children when the old leave. I pulled out my sweet tooth and dug in, mugging for cameras, feeling sick. My mind was already forming the new self that could drop into her life.

What I learned first at the arboretum:

For most plants, cross-pollination began as a mistake. A bee discovered nectar at the base of the flower and carried pollen from one plant to another. The cross-pollinated flowers then created stronger, more diverse seeds that created more colorful and fragrant flowers. This works for the bees because they are able to find the nectar more quickly, and it works for the flowers because this method produces healthier plants.

There are also plants that depend only on the wind to do this work. These plants have longer stamen and pistols. They are dull, with little to no fragrance and no need for petals. They don't need to attract animals or insects and are content to allow the non-biased work of the wind to create next year's seed.

I have always been the wind-pollinated plant. I prefer to allow motion to decide. My choice is to stay rooted, to allow this, to hide him.

I never had the desire to be a care-giver. For my dogs, sure, but not another person. This is somehow different. I walk up the

e guest bedroom. The door is open a crack so I push
a little further and look in. He is resting with his eyes
sed. The dogs have joined him on the bed. He hears me and
turns his head, opens his eyes. The dogs don't bother to move.

"What's your name?" he asks, his clear eyes on me.

"Corbina," I say and look down, suddenly feeling like a child.
It's a childish name, girly, one that makes me blush in front of
men when I say it.

"Do people call you Bina for short?" He smiles, his large ears
move a little with that movement.

"No, I've never been called anything but my full name."

"Okay, Corbina. It's unusual—a family name?"

"No, I don't—My mother…" I search for words and fail.

"I was named after my grandfather," he says. I'm not sure why
this surprises me, this small average thing. I guess it's because
he arrived with such a blank history. I wonder if he has remembered anything else. I don't ask.

"If you get hungry, come get me. I'll make us both something to eat." I leave the room feeling embarrassed.

Once downstairs I don't know what to do with myself. More
clouds have moved in, making the afternoon even darker. It
starts to snow again, but not heavily. I rub my face, first making
circles over my eyes and then moving out to cover the whole
thing with my hands. It feels good to manipulate the muscles
in my face, to try to release some tension. I have no idea how to
spend time with someone else in the house.

Her feet in slippers on the stairs. Dragging them, scuffing the heel with tired steps. She must have heard the dogs. This morning has been coming for some time and is now starting a series of movements toward a standoff, toward the natural resistance to interruption.

I cannot help but smile as she steps into view. Sleep heavy and knotted hair. She pulls her robe tighter around her hipless waist. She looks stunned. She will not let me interrupt.

She begins her morning by cracking eggs, the flick of a browned wrist breaking them open, tossing the shells, a quick movement of a sharp knife and the ripping sound it makes as it passes through green onions, then nearly silent as it passes through mushrooms. She stands at the counter watching me.

"Hello Corbina," I want to say. But I am mute, like my daughter Sarah, controlling things by making the other person overact, over think. I am willing to wait. I wait.

I decide to finish sewing curtains for my bedroom. It will force me to focus on measurement and straight lines. I set up the machine and pull out the semi-sheer fabric I bought a few years ago. When placing the pins, I prefer a slight prick to the safety of a thimble. The machine's light clicks on and then starts its whirring. I look up to watch the last few yellow aspen leaves dislodge from their branch. I have to rip the seam.

The curtains are finished after several distracted passes. I have to force them onto the rod, which is no surprise since I eye-balled it. Light passes through the pale cream of the fabric. It's satisfying to have them finished; a task I have put off and put off. Martin's presence creates a nervous energy I fill by making chicken stock to freeze, by cleaning out drawers in the kitchen, and scrubbing baseboards—all in the same afternoon. I search things out, one after the other, to avoid his company. Normally I would have sat around on a cold Saturday, flipping through seed catalogs, creating wish lists of bizarre vegetables. I have a new book to read on *companion planting,* about which plants should be in the same bed because they have properties that help each other thrive. It's fascinating, but it doesn't hold my attention today. Martin must be conscious of my movement through the house, though he hasn't come out of the guest room.

My lunch is made, eaten. I take him a sandwich. He eats it on the bed while absorbing the weak sun. The dogs go out and come in. The same routine on this different day.

Around 4:00 he finds me in an armchair by the fire, repairing a small hole in a pair of work jeans. He hands me a twenty. *Where did that come from?* I hold the bill in the air between us.

"What's this for?"

"Groceries. I'd like some bacon. Whatever else you want, get."

I am happy at the suggestion to leave the house and put together a quick list in my head. I add men's socks to the mental note, maybe slippers—the house has original windows: there is plastic over most of them, but that only does so much.

"Okay," I say and get up, leaving quickly, shutting myself into the car and watching the white exhaust as I let the engine warm.

I find a parking space in a far corner and then make my way through the slush, push into the warmth of the store, the stale smell of plastic-wrapped meats and produce from other continents. I select good rolls for our breakfast tomorrow, some celery and carrots—feel that quick shame of not selecting organic—and some chuck to cut up into stew meat. I love the ritual of making it, the smell of the carrots, celery, and onions as they simmer in butter and oil. I love pressing each cube of meat onto a towel to rid it of moisture and then browning the meat in a pan. I love how slow cooking fills the house with warmth. I find his bacon. It seems expensive and a small moment of guilt pulses through me. I haven't had bacon in years. Years. I pay and then walk up the sidewalk of the strip mall.

∾

I wander through the men's department, touch flannel shirts, stiff button downs and slim cut blazers. My own clothing comes from Salvation Army, from anonymous men. I never lock myself into dressing rooms and admire the fit or cut of clothing. I make a guess by holding the clothes up to my body, always erring on the bigger side. For Martin, I select large white socks with gold toes, a pair of green slippers, and a pack of white undershirts. I have the idea older men still wear them, and layers in my house are a necessity. I pay for these things with the twenty he gave me and watch for looks from the cashier. I'm over-thinking things, of course. No cashier is going to think twice about a woman buying these items. It's still the newness that keeps me on edge and makes me feel like I'm being watched with suspicion. I look forward to presenting Martin with these tokens of thoughtfulness.

Outside, the snow, again, coming down still stronger. I anticipate the fire at home, the dogs, the man. There will be dinner at the table, not the couch, and with company other than my dogs.

Around the time she asked me about her name, Corbina started asking her grandmother about her father. She wanted to know what he looked like in case they passed in the grocery store or on the sidewalk. My mom knew nothing about him. I never told her.

She made up stories for Corbina about his height and eye color. She talked about how he was doing Peace Corps work in some remote place when they lost track of him. She wanted the loss of him to be less personal—what I mean is that she wanted the loss to not be a choice. She wanted to make the larger world to blame. I couldn't let that happen. The loss was mine, too, after all.

I told Corbina her father wasn't dead or missing and that his eyes weren't even grey, like hers. I don't know what she believes because she stopped asking. All the details about him became suspect.

What I could offer were alternatives to our peaceful, if just functional, home. I left case files on the kitchen table, knowing Corbina would read them. I told her about confidentiality and the protocols for anonymity. I made it easy for her to be interested.

I understand now those files were a bad idea. There were plenty of fathers, uncles, and older brothers in them. There were lots of mothers in the "impaired care-giver" category. I had hoped she would compare me and find me adequate. I didn't think too much about the harm they could do, like a contact trauma. I could be reading into it now, of course. I can't ask her about them; we've never talked about if she actually read them or not. I'm sure she did. How could she resist? I couldn't, not at her age. How can I tell how much pulling away from the world was my fault?

She moved out as soon as she could and worked strange hours and lived in basement apartments until she saved up enough to buy a small farm house. I told co-workers how proud I was to have such an independent daughter and how so many kids don't bother to get their own places anymore. I was surprised when she became a person person, not just a version of me. She decided to do manual labor and work outdoors. She told me about moving out of my house, she didn't ask if it was okay. I was surprised to have her stay in the same town, though. She stayed close enough to maintain a true distance—the possibility of weekend dinners that rarely happened.

I am always surprised by her hands and how sun-beaten they are, her nails clean but stained from dirt. She drives when we go somewhere on rare weekends and I watch her hands touch the wheel like the points of a compass on a sheet of paper, exact but without pressure, a clear purpose in their stiffness.

The dogs greet me at the door, as always, when I return. Their wild eyes and legs bring an immediate smile to my face. I let them outside and they tumble into each other, play biting and rolling around. I watch them a moment longer before closing the door and unpacking the groceries. I leave the ingredients for the stew on the counter.

I climb the stairs to find Martin and give him the socks, slippers and undershirts I bought for him. The guest room is empty. I knock on the bathroom. No response. I look out the upstairs hall window to see if there are footprints in the backyard. Nothing—the snow is clean and unbroken. I feel my pulse in my chest as I travel back downstairs. I feel less worried than irrationally abandoned.

"Martin?" I call down the steps to the basement—the only other place he could be. I drop the bag of clothing at the foot of the stairs and then open the front door. The dogs push in, cold and wet. They shake and spray a fine mist over the hallway. Standing in the doorframe, I feel the temperature change on my skin.

"He's gone," I say. I sit on a stool at the counter and look at the bright red meat in its tight plastic wrap.

"Corbina," he says from over my shoulder. Martin is at the top of the stairs that lead to the basement.

I startle and then let my face fall, let any emotion fall.

"Those are for you." I point at the bag near his feet and then move around to the other side of the counter.

I rip into the plastic and begin pressing the blood and moisture from the meat.

She came home earlier than expected. I was in the basement when I heard the front door open, followed by the crush of plastic bags and the dog's feet sliding on the linoleum. I could have moved quickly up the stairs and talked about helping with the laundry, except I had only the clothes I was wearing. I just kept quiet, listening to her unpack the groceries and talk nonsense to the dogs. I heard her leave the first floor.

What could I have been doing down here? I looked around. A second hand couch with threadbare arms, yellow plaid and deep body imprints. A cabinet. A washer and dryer. It was too much home for one person, but who should deny a want?

Corbina approached the basement and called down, my name rising a little in her mouth, making it a question: Martin?

I hear her sit at the table and then I climb the steps.

"Corbina."

She turns to see me. I watch it all and smile.

"I'm right here. Did you think I left?"

"I wasn't sure."

She looks down and then over to a plastic bag near the steps.

I open the bag and see socks, green corduroy slippers and a packet of white undershirts.

I sit down and snap open the plastic ring that holds the socks together and then slide a pair on. Warmth, finally. The slippers are a little snug, but they will stretch to meet my feet. I leave the undershirts on the table.

"Thank you. My feet feel better."

"You're welcome," she says, stands.

She begins chopping carrots, her posture perfect, shoulders lined up, rough fingers moving over the orange taproot, making it smaller with each downward pass of the knife. She looks up and meets my eyes, then looks down to her cutting board. I understand. She wants me to leave the room.

I walk slowly to the stairs, grasp the banister, and haul myself up to the bed.

She is a stranger woman than I had imagined.

She didn't yell, didn't question me about what I was doing in the basement. She gave me socks even though I stepped on our strange arrangement. She offered me gifts picked out for the old confused man, not a stranger in the basement.

What do you know about me, Corbina? I am an old man you found in your field. I am your stray dog, your secret.

I hear the chopping again and smell the way each vegetable softens, the changes of texture and taste. I can smell the celery becoming translucent.

Mom visits on Sunday, like we agreed. I ask Martin to stay in the guest bedroom with the door locked. I ask that he try not to move around. This seemed to make him happy, but maybe I read too much into his expression. He seemed tired.

She arrives a little early with a library book on résumé building.

"Hi, Mom," I say as I open the door.

"Hello." She smiles and gestures for me to help her with the book and the coffee cake she's carrying.

She takes off her coat and hat and shakes out her hair, tries to remove its flatness. The house feels strange because of Martin's hidden presence. Call it paranoia, a hyper awareness of environment. Mom and I move into the kitchen. I get two small plates and start some water for tea. Mom opens the drawer that holds the knives and then cuts two generous pieces of coffee cake. We sit and wait for the water to boil.

"How are you?" I watch her eyebrows as she smiles.

"Pretty good. I had a cough, from the weather, but it seems to be okay." She seems smaller today and I don't like it. Vulnerability doesn't suit her. She doesn't ask back, doesn't ask how I'm doing. I offer it, though, to keep the conversation moving.

"I'm doing well. I sold the last of my acorn squash last weekend." I keep going, trying to avoid any lapse, any moment of hesitation. "A groundhog made his way into the greenhouse, tunneled in and pushed aside the bricks. There's nothing to eat in there, not now. Next season though."

"Get a bb gun and scare them with a little shot."

"I'd try smoke bombs first!" I know better than to be surprised, but I can't help it. I try to keep the judgment from my face.

The kettle sounds; I rise to turn it off and pour water into two mugs. With the tea now steeping, we begin to take bites of the cake. It's delicious—brown sugar and butter. I use the back of my fork to collect the crumbs, pressing them into the tines.

"I brought that book for you. You can keep yourself clean and work inside."

"I have a job I like. I have a house. I have dogs." They lift their heads and look at me in anticipation. *And now Martin.*

I call the dogs over and scratch their necks. They wag and shift their weight around, try to get me to hit the right spot. Mom smiles, she does like them but would never consider caring for a dog.

Martin is silent upstairs.

"I'm not tired of gardening, not at all. I don't know if you understand what I do all day."

Mom continues to chew and I realize she hasn't heard me. I follow her line of sight to the basement steps. A sock, a man's sock. She is silent in her pride about knowing something, even if she doesn't exactly know what that something means. I sip at the tea, first blowing on the surface.

"Are you finished?" I ask and pick up her plate. The hard crumb topping she saves for last, still uneaten.

"I'm no—well." She puts her fork down and wipes her lips with a napkin.

I scrape the toping into the trash and then slide the dish into the sink.

Leave this alone, I want to say. *Leave it alone.* I don't say anything as I finish my tea, as she adds more milk to lower the temperature of hers. We each remain in this tight circle of restraint.

Can I tell her she disappoints me? Is that possible, to say that? To tell her would invite her reflection; she would show me myself, and my disappointments.

At least I gave her that space. At least I never asked her to tell me more about herself. Did I wish she would? Of course. Did I wish she had more drive, more ambitions. Yes. But how could I make her feel guilty?

From what I understand, she does garden with talent. Maybe I never told her. We move in uncertain orbits, unsure who is the planet and who is the moon.

How could I not be defensive about her father? How could I explain why I was ready to accept so little affection? I could tell her the last thing her father said to me. Well, that and the second to last thing. His hand was on her head, her just-born head. He looked at her and said, "I made that." Then his eyes went to mine and he corrected himself.

"We made that."

He looked at her again, removed his hand from her head. It

was the last sentence I heard from him, the last time I saw him. I heard secondhand about where he was living and with whom. I didn't follow up. I wasn't concerned about keeping it going. I had Corbina.

She leaves the house after the tense breakfast. I watch her walk to the greenhouse, her feet heavy in the snow. I open the drawers in the kitchen, in her bedroom, her study. There are small objects hidden away. A dried orange peel in the round shape of its missing fruit, mystic texts with underlines, a gray silk scarf with sweat stains. I mourn the smallness of her experience. I find other things, truly private things: my need to absorb like a dirty sponge, a steady opening of envelopes with other's names, the private sound of a body in the bathtub, turning to submerge the other hip, the cold hip of a narrow tub, an egret taken from its stillness, plucked by its thin neck—the feeling of opening her drawers and cabinets, that private stillness and so thin a strategy for invisibility. Brigit, her mother: anger and satisfaction. I take them in, learning and categorizing Corbina's life. An ear turned for the sound of the door.

After she leaves, I climb the steps to his room. I knock on the locked door.

"She's gone," I say to the wood.

He opens the door and returns to the bed. With effort he lifts the weight of his long legs to recline.

"How did it go?" His face is tired but full of disobedience. He is handsome.

"She saw your sock on the step. She knows about you."

"Well, she doesn't know about me, just someone in her mind. Did she say anything?"

"Of course not! I caught her looking away, lost in her head. I leaned over to see what she was looking at, and there it was on the third step, covered in dog hair."

"But she didn't ask? How are you sure she knew it was a man's? How do you know she knows it wasn't your sock? Are you making too much of it—filling in the details for her?"

"Definitely not. She was excited. She wouldn't look at me directly."

"All it means is your mother thinks you've had someone over. Someone who slept over or maybe just removed his shoes. That you have a boyfriend." His big ears move up his head as he smiles.

I raise my eyebrows. "Boyfriend? Nothing is private with her. The last thing I want to do is explain you. She won't ask. That's the thing. We don't talk, not about anything like that."

"Nothing to worry about, then. I'll keep a closer watch on my socks." He looks me in the face.

"Okay?"

I am not smiling, but I am slightly relieved. Martin picks up my book about the hemispheres. I watch his eyes move across the pages.

I want to say something like *we don't have a plan*. But I don't have a plan; I hate the impulse toward order, but I revert to it when it comes to my mom. I know what Martin doesn't. The next time she visits she will be searching for another *something*: a toothbrush, fine-toothed comb, a slight tobacco smell from the trash can. It's time for diligence. She'll be over more often.

I let my eyes close. Apple crisp tomorrow. Curried butternut soup. Kale. My mind turns to menus when stressed. Brown sugar, oat, root cellar vegetables, turmeric. Cooking for two is slightly better than cooking for one.

I saw this part of her, the part she will not recognize. I am surprised she caved so quickly. Her mother. I overheard her ask her mother if she had heard anything about a lost man. Who looks for a lost man? Lost women are something to worry about, not men. Even ones who have left a family behind. A wife, a daughter, a son. They will not look for me. No one would bother.

When she was twenty, she had a job paving and repaving the same road for six months. Every day Corbina and the other people on road crew blocked a hilly and shaded stretch of road between two major through-streets on the edge of town. Every day they back-hoed up the fresh asphalt they laid down the day before. They were after the pipes under the street but no one could tell what they were doing or why, day after day, they needed to access this vein. The workers took turns standing at either end of the work site, holding alternating *slow* and *stop* signs as people braked sharply to avoid collisions. After all, it was a daily surprise they hadn't finished. How could this work go on for so long?

Corbina never talked about her work. I knew she operated the forklift that slid giant slabs of metal over the open hole, slabs that were then asphalted into place so traffic could make its bumpy way over them.

"When are you going to be finished that job?" I'd ask her.

She would shrug, "When it's done."

"Isn't it boring? Going over the same part every day?"

She never answered questions like that because they were just too dull. It was difficult to make conversation because there were so many times in an hour she became silent, expecting you to answer your own question and also create the next topic of conversation. And then there were things I could never talk about, like anything personal. Even the slightest thing, like a bandage on her hand—if I were to ask how she hurt herself, the question could result in a cold silence that would last weeks.

I wonder at the attraction and if attraction is the right word for it. The obsession was not physical, although I couldn't protest all possibilities. I laugh at myself: my old body in bed, layers of quilts, layers of socks. I imagine her sliding in next to me and feeling her warmth. How tame and sentimental I have gotten.

My wife and I had twenty years together. It was a second marriage for both of us. It had been a good match, produced two children, both of whom were in college. When they left for school we were alone in the house for the first time. We had long talks about how each of us had moved into another's apartment after high school and how what we knew of ourselves was always in relation to other people, our spouses, our children, and, earlier— our parents and families.

There were no infidelities, no bankruptcies, no addictions. None of the things that make people break down or run away.

And still, when I left, I felt like my place in that home had been transient, always transient. My role was to pass through.

That's not to say I didn't love them.

The steps of a circle have taken me here.

My wife and I used to drop acid and ride the bus from one end of the line to the other. We had to pay the fare again at that point. We were the only two onboard, in a strange part of the westernmost edge. We'd walk up to the driver, put our money in the machine, and sit back down near the back of the bus. People came on, we listened and slid our shoes over the sticky floor, the stiffness of strychnine creeping into our muscles and back.

These moments were what we would reference later, after the kids had come. In bed, my wife would turn to me and say, an imp, a character from that bus ride:

"Hey little man, wipe your nose. Wipe your nose, little man. Little man, wipe it." One of the ways we found connection.

I don't have to ask him not to leave because he doesn't want to go anywhere. His captivity speaks of an omission about life before he came here, a life I understand he is hiding from me. We haven't talked about it beyond the first morning when I asked him about calling a family. I understand now that he remembers his life before here and his home or homelessness, his life alone. He remembers a phone number, his age, his shoe size—many numbers. He knew them and withheld them. I fill in his story, working backwards from the night in the field.

Shoeless? No good answer for that. It stays in the grey area of trauma. He must be a widower because of how comfortable he is in the home, with me feeding him. He had shared his space with a woman. He knew her breakfast and the scraping of crumbs from the table into his cupped palm. And the night fire seemed habitual. I had never fallen into these rituals of time spent with another. To couple up is a way to keep static and not develop, a way to keep a moment of clarity, only a moment, of clarity repeating each day. A place held at the table.

Did I know that I was the type of person to get angry over newspapers spread all over the house, that I would come home and straighten them, fold them back up and add them to the recycling without saying a word? Did I know I would leave notes in the bathroom about not leaving globs of toothpaste in the sink? It doesn't matter that I now know this about myself. Knowing does not change anything. It is the same as not knowing, collecting the newspapers is the same as not spreading them around the house in the first place. The end is the same.

His gender and age—a lifetime of gathered habits all pointing back at me, showing me my own gender and age and habits. I accumulated these habits in isolation and did not always enjoy learning just how cut off I had been.

His past. A widower, but not a father. I often watch him after he has fallen asleep in front of the fire, the dogs at his feet and a book in his lap. I try to see children and their first days at school. I try to imagine a house full of miniature things—shoes, pants, elephants. I try to imagine the hurt a parent experiences when their children reject them. I'm not sure how this would show in his sleeping face, but I look anyway. He looks younger by at least a few years when sleeping, a fairly common thing, I think, because the muscles relax and worry lines become less pronounced, the frown lines become softer. The more I look, the more certain I become of his story: his wife of many years had died a slow death. He moved from their house into an apartment. He adjusted to the smallness of his new life. He retired, collected Social Security. No pension? What work did he do? Impossible to imagine him in an office. This part of his history doesn't interest me anyway. I have never driven myself hard enough to wedge into one thing or another. My job at the arboretum is enough—a place where I could see the results of my efforts.

Everything in his life had been a march toward this. I was grateful to feel this, to feel the weight of caring for another person.

Sometimes I rewrite things. I had called 9-1-1 and reported that a confused barefoot man was walking in the field across my house. I had watched their approach, lights but no sirens. I had watched them wrap him in thick brown blankets and wheel him into the back of the ambulance. I saw silhouettes taking his blood pressure and temperature. Finally, I had watched them secure the gurney and shut the double doors. I write in feelings of relief and pride about doing the right thing. I saved him from frostbite, worse. I imagine going to bed, turning off the light, and then waking to the same world I had known.

I try to let myself think of how pleased I am to have him staying with me, how it is temporary and how eventually I will notify someone. Am I so insensitive as to keep him? Maybe he has a brother or sister. Maybe he has his wife's gravestone to visit. What about when he dies? How would I hide that? How would I bury him? I would have to bring people into my home to take him away and record his death, to make documents certifying it. I would need to explain that I don't know his last name or if the first name I call him is really his. I will need to explain why I didn't call the police when I found him wandering.

I already imagine my life without him and how I will be changed by his leaving. I try to remember that everything is the same, will be the same, that knowing him is the same as the not knowing him.

My grandmother's closets were still full of her husband's clothing. I had never met him; he passed away or left, it wasn't clear, before I was born. The stiff pants and pressed shirts were horrifying. The penny loafers and folded sweaters, ties hung on the back of the closet door. She didn't even see them anymore; they were just part of the door. She walked past them to get her own clothing. My mother saw them, though. She demanded that her mother donate the clothing and offered to bag it up. She offered to take a few of the nicer pieces to a consignment shop.

Grandmother would then close the door to the closet and then the door to the bedroom, shuttling us out, muttering words in another language. She and my mother were trapped. I escaped them by walking my grandmother's dog. When I returned, red-cheeked and winded, the women would be sitting together at the table having coffee. They had moved on but kept their grief ready to replay.

I would be upset with my mother and confused by my grandmother. Why would she insist on getting rid of her father's things? Why were his things the only things they would talk about on these visits? There was a picture of a dark haired man on my grandmother's dresser. My mom couldn't look at the pictures. I wasn't sure if she was aware of her avoidance. Her aversion made me focus on the picture. I would end up holding it and asking about him. The photo had been retouched with blue in his eyes and blush on his cheeks.

"His eyes weren't blue, they were hazel," she told me. "The army airbrushed them in these things." She would take the photo and put it back in its place. And that was it.

But, Martin, his silence was endearing because it allowed me to create his story. I was able to craft the person who sat across from me, the person who ate all that was put in front of him, made me cook even better meals, and put on a little happy weight.

I sometimes wished he would ask me more about myself, but, whenever he did, I shut down, afraid he wouldn't like the answers. I was afraid he would judge me in some way. I wanted us to agree to never apologize. Apologizing meant someone had been misunderstood. I wanted only clarity, even if that meant we created the other person's intentions in our heads. It was real enough.

I notice a man's sock on the basement steps. It's a single sock that must have fallen out of a basket of laundry on the its way to the washer. I try not to look at it too often as we sit together at the kitchen table. But I can't help it. Corbina follows my eyes. She knows I won't ask, but is angry I know something of her private life.

We finish our small meal and begin to straighten up, get ready to leave the house together. She stalls for a moment, tells me to go ahead. I'm sure she throws the sock the rest of the way down the stairs to the basement. She meets my eyes on the porch, silences any impulse in me to ask.

I turn the radio on. People were arguing about intent.

"What are they talking about, really?" I ask her. "What will be different tomorrow?" I ask her.

She is silent. The car passes the fields around her home. Everything is layered in white. I watch her listening to the newscast. Her sun-beaten hands are stiff on the wheel. We are going to a movie. It is one we would never have watched alone.

The theater will be like this car. We will be sitting next to each other while other people's words create noise around us.

It is hardest to watch her hardness and know I shaped it. I know that my unhappiness increases without the wall of her resistance. She knows this and keeps her face still. She pretends to be passive.

What I imagined about my father:

Dark hair

Dark eyes

Tall, like bone aches, like collapsed shoulders to hide his height

A thick bottom lip

What I knew about when I was born:

My mom shaved off her eyebrows and drew them in, hair by hair. Her makeup bag was from then on full of pencils. She had a terror of discontinuation. Her arches were perfect, realistic, and never made of hair again.

What I imagined:

He was still alive.

What I knew:

That she learned to wipe me clean of him. I used to believe I could be satisfied just holding something of his. A ring, a money clip, a religious medallion of a favorite saint. Anything that had spent time in the warmth of his closed palm. I taught myself not to ask why he wasn't curious about me—the same gnaw of every fatherless child.

What hard pounding thoughts of Corbina up to the day I arrived. The watching of weather forecasts, first weekly, then daily, and then, on the day of, hourly. I was aiming for snow and the weatherman was stage director, telling me when to enter. I left the house without a coat, but with shoes.

My family, of course, wasn't home. I scanned each room before I left, looking for things to form memories around.

A signed baseball from my youth. I picked up a statue of a saint to find the coin my wife placed under it. My daughter's room and the guitar that had been my sister's and was now hers. Her closet door was open and showed folded jeans that didn't fit her anymore. I once saw the tops of a six-pack of beer between their folds, but didn't worry about her drinking the beer, not warm like that. She needed private things the same way I did. It was more about the taking something from me than a desire for drunkenness.

My son's room only needed the slightest of looks, my eyes going right for the picture of him and his core group of friends—

burned noses, bleached hair, on the dock at the lake. They are stunning in their happiness.

Keys? Do I take them? If I take them I can lock the door behind me. If I leave them my wife would think I intended to be right back.

I could not stand the idea of an intruder, even though I wouldn't be there to see what he took. I knew the chances of this happening were next to none, but I locked the door anyway.

Down the stairs to the backyard. I lift one of the slate stones of the walkway and make a shallow hole. I drop my keys in and cover them up, replace the stone.

I started the walk, head down, shoulders up near my ears, the wind at my neck. I walk quickly, cutting through yards, using paths known to mailmen. I was at her home before I was ready, before it was snowing. I waited by an irrigation tunnel, protected by the wind. I waited until the flurries started, until the ground was covered.

I unlaced my shoes and slid them from my feet, pulled off my socks and tucked them into the toes of the shoes, the toes pointing south, a neat pair. I thought of nothing but the steps. I found a pattern to count.

I could barely contain a familiar greeting.

He sometimes calls the dogs by the wrong names, like he did the night he met them. He sometimes overreacts to small things, like when the pasta was too hot to eat right away. He reacted like a child.

These behaviors started in earnest after I found his newspaper clippings. Or maybe I just noticed the reactions more, they brought more attention to themselves.

I had been sweeping the dog hair from baseboards in his room when I noticed a newspaper clipping caught between the drawers of his bedside table. I reached for it instinctively, my first thought was to just push it all the way into the drawer so it didn't fall out or rip. But the stronger instinct, curiosity, took over. I wanted to see what he had torn so carefully from the paper.

It was from the section that featured local sports. A boy swimmer had qualified for a conference championship. Nothing remarkable. I opened the drawer further and found two more clippings; these included an announcement about a girl passing the bar exam and another about the boy going to finals.

I had expected, somehow, to see a police blotter with a missing persons mention. I thought—all in that moment of hesitation, that moment when I decided to snoop—maybe I would find out his last name, his age and a former address. Some of the mundane details of life that nonetheless mean something.

I found a family. His children! I had been so certain he didn't have any. I put the papers back as I found them, the one with the boy sticking up and out of the drawer. I wondered if their placement had been deliberate and if he had set me up. Did he place the clipping in such a way as to make it impossible for me to ignore? Did he place them in some silent way to monitor their movement, to know if they had been disturbed?

I decided not give anything away. I was determined to make sure this wouldn't change anything for me.

A family hidden in a drawer. How could I not care?

Some part of me has grown more dependent on Martin's presence in my life. The clippings showed me something outside of the story I created. I decided to protect him from the newspaper's influence. I told him I had plans to stop the subscription.

My wife had a different idea of work. I needed a job. I needed to do a job, get promoted, move forward. She did not need a job to be part of the world. She seemed more authentic, untied to an occupation. I wanted this freedom. It's not like I had *a calling*.

How do people say, I am going to be a doctor?

Parents were doctors or some such thing. Mostly. Some sort of edge.

Work makes me angry, even now. I do not miss the run of the neighborhoods.

At first after retirement, I was ecstatic to shape my days in whatever way they fell together. Then I realized I got up at the same time every day without setting an alarm.

Kitchen, coffee, newspaper, meal.

The same, daily, but I had to draw things out, stretch them so as not to create another something to do.

I watched my wife fill her days.

Up earlier, small chores first, then a breakfast after mine and whatever coffee I left in the pot.

I would follow her around the house. I was surprised when she left for such long stretches. At work I always imagined her home, although I never thought about what she would have been doing there.

Alone for most of the day. It was the same, the same as working.

I looked for another job. Greeter at a box store. Library help desk. School cafeteria. What jobs were open to old men.

I didn't want them. I applied for them all and became a greeter.

I worked for two weeks without telling my wife. I quit without telling her.

The routes I did all those years—paths worn into front yards from my shoes—I started them again.

People would see me pass their mailbox and come out to check, then look up the street toward me, close the box and go back inside.

It was strange to be recognized outside of a uniform.

I needed to have a secret. I needed to guard something and worry about it.

Part of me understands I was lucky to have one parent rather than two. The same part of me celebrated loss because I knew it was wrong. I've been satisfied with so little. I was free from a father's influence, except I wasn't.

I want to know why she hasn't been married. Everyone has been married at least once. I want this explanation from her. She doesn't answer. She wants to know how I know she hasn't.

"He moved out?" I ask. I cause a small hurt, a fissure.

I realize her mother must have given her these same small hurts.

Corbina is immune.

No. There has never been a he here.

She reaches out with her right hand, slowly, deliberately, and removes my glasses. She folds the temples of the frames and tucks them into the front pocket of her shirt before standing to leave the table. The words in the book I hold now illegible.

She doesn't push in her chair.

I watch her back as she turns the corner to ascend the stairs.

I purchased new flannel button-downs and two pairs of jeans. I did not buy him shoes. I picked up two packets of plaid boxers, three blue t-shirts and a pair of pajama pants. He hadn't asked for any of it. The purchases came organically out of need. I realized he slept in his jeans after their sleep-sweat smell hit as he walked to the kitchen table for breakfast. He never mentioned needing anything.

He says, "We wear the same kind of shirts. Nearly the same size, even though they're huge on you."

I look down at my thin flannel and then back up at Martin.

"I guess so."

"Why do you dress that way, like a man? You can dress whatever way you want—but, how come?"

"I just like it. It's easier."

"You hide yourself."

I look at his face. He is doing his best to appear neutral, like an observer and not someone with some sort of agenda.

"I'm not hiding. I just like things big." I raise my arms in a sort of flapping way, to demonstrate ease of movement. I realize I look stupid and stop, fold my arms across my chest.

"You should take me out shopping and I'll pick something out for you."

We both raise our eyebrows, knowing both things would never happen.

"This shirt is feminine. It has pearly buttons."

He smiles a full, genuine smile.

Mom visits with a gun. It's a small one used by boys to shoot birds and feral cats.

"This is for your groundhog," she says and starts to hand it over. She sees my disapproval.

"I'll take care of it you need me to."

I take the gun from her. I would find her stalking my yard with it if I didn't take it.

"I don't need you to take care of them. They aren't around now, anyway. Nothing is growing.

"I'll be ready this spring," she says. She puts her hat and gloves down on the hall table. We haven't moved further into the house and I don't plan on inviting her in the rest of the way. I don't want her near the house, not now that I'm anticipating her eyes searching for any small sign of another person.

"Where did you get it?"

"A friend."

A friend, I think. *What friends does she have?*

She's come over just after dinner so we could do our grocery shopping together. Both of us hate the task even though I love cooking and she loves to bake. We are better at being mother and daughter during visits with clear purposes and time constraints.

"How's work?" I ask her as we start our drive.

"Busy," she says. I know she wants to talk about it, so I wait for her to continue. She is distracted, though. She seems to be looking out the window, but I know she is deep in her head. I don't know what I expect her to say.

We pull up to the supermarket and each grab a cart. I take out the list Martin gave me. It's full of random things, like jerky. I've never bought it and am not sure where to even find it in the store. I wonder if my mom will notice how varied my cart is. She doesn't. This is the first time I've paid much attention to what she has put in hers.

I see Martin's figure move through the front hall as we pull into the driveway. I feel my cheeks fill their capillaries. I know I have to offer her tea and invite her in. It's what we do. We get out of my car and then transfer her groceries from my trunk to hers. It's cold enough not to worry about them. I linger by my car, shift my bags from hip to hip.

"Coming?" she says from the front porch. She hasn't offered to help carry anything. She waits under the dim light.

"Here's the key," I say and awkwardly try to move it close enough for her to grab. She takes it from my hand.

The gun isn't on the hall table. From the stairs, I see Martin's door is open. I hurry to the kitchen to unpack, put the kettle on.

The water is rushed into tea, the tea weakly steeped and then gulped. We say our goodbyes.

I close and lock the front door.

"Martin!" I yell once her car is down the driveway.

He comes up the basement steps holding the gun.

"Neat little set up," he says and cocks the gun's small hammer. He fires it into the floor of the hall closet and then hands it to me.

There is a cloud of sulfur smoke rising to the bedrooms. There are tiny holes in the floor. The dogs whimper and then bark.

Captain Beefheart. The 13th Floor Elevators, my internal rhythm, the clock I set my body's electricity to.

It was endless, this supply of questions and doubts.

Doubts, I loved them. My wife did not. As would anyone trying to live with another. They are impossible to give yourself over to—to doubt you made the right choice in marriage, in children.

Yes, let's go with droning drums and tinny, repetitive guitar lines.

I add things to the grocery list:

Two bottles of red. Anything but Shiraz.

Xanax. (I know, get a prescription, please. Tell the doc about your trouble sleeping, your anxiety—tell a story for me. Lately the walls come in when I speak: a black tunnel of panic. I have learned to talk myself down, to convince myself my mouth is not full of gibberish, my brain and mouth meeting in the usual way—I see what your body says and go from there. Your face tells me I am making sense when I speak. Please.)

Duck: dark meat, fat-rich. Taste the seasons and the brevity of their lives.

Celery, when simmered with carrots and onions, the holy trinity—mirepoix—is the only smell that describes safety and domesticity. Celery, that fibrous plant with so little taste until it meets heat.

Dog treats.

A fox pup stared me down the other day. I was outdoors, not allowed in this current exile. At first, I couldn't make out what it was. It stood in the road, between Corbina's driveway and the field. I thought it was a cat, then a puppy and finally a fox. I was maybe a hundred feet away when it crossed the street and ran behind the house. I followed it and waited and saw it move through our backyard, pausing to stop and sniff the bench that was never used. Corbina was not even aware of the bench anymore, not in the sitting sense, only in the accomplishment sense, as in, *I bought that wood and metal, cemented it there, in that corner of the yard.* The pup raised his eyes and met mine and held them, then lowered his head and skulked away.

And, I think, I'm sleeping tonight. With dogs curled around my feet and the moon on my thinning hair, the white light on my pillow, my lunacy full.

My cousin, the outlaw, writes me notes and leaves them under the doormat. I am unsure how he knows I am here or why I thought to check under the mat. I am sure my wife and children do not know I am in the same town, that we are sharing a zip code. He and I were born on the same day, a year apart. We have not been able to split our lives.

Sun-dried tomatoes, why not?

Jerky. I lost a tooth to its tough smokiness. Where I grew up they sold it in great slabs. It was an after school ritual to purchase the edible leather. I wonder about the smallness of that town's grocery store and the cashier. About her memory of food routines: steak night for this woman, frozen lasagna for that man, crates of pudding for that family.

I notice a small dark mound under the eye of one of the dogs. It is a growth, full of dark blood. I squeeze it one afternoon and it fills up the next day. The dog's face is white under the eyes and along the snout. Even his feet have gotten lighter with age. I wonder at this bleaching of the dog, the bleaching and washing out of life.

I had to drive past Corbina's house on the way to a home visit. A waterlogged teenage mother needed help with her red-haired son. He spits in women's eyes like some kind of lizard. I slowed to observe my daughter's dark windows, windows that took years of nagging to cover with drapes, and when she broke down and bought the material—dark like bruised fruit—she admitted she became a better neighbor once they were up. *Like a slip that protects the gap of light between legs. Like that*, she said. She had been content to have the blindness of interior light, confident no one was interested in her, that no one even noticed she lived there as she moved room to room unseen. The purple drapes were drawn. The mail hadn't come yet; the red flag on her mailbox was up. The snow is pushed off her driveway into the street, a salt-crusted blue.

My client, the young mother, lives with her parents in a small house in a new development. The soil there can barely support grass. I pull into her driveway. The mother is at the door with the child on her hip. She is letting the snow blow past them into the house. She does not wave or acknowledge I'm there. Both her and her child's cheeks are red. The child has a thin crust of mucus covering a nostril. She pushes the door open a little further and then leaves her post. The heat blows from the vents in the floor and moves her hair a little as she paces.

"Let me hold him."

She gives him over and then turns on the TV. We sit together like this for some time. The child, having a rare nap, breathes heavily from his mouth. I look away from his face and at the girl's profile.

"When did he last spit?"

She turns to face me—her contemptible family support worker—and takes a long look at my grey hair. I recently had it cut and feel confident about its shape, but her stare makes me uneasy; I push the longer front pieces behind my ears. I imagine the neatness of my bob makes her self-conscious about her own hair. She has a line of pale ash blonde roots next to the length's saturation of black dye. Her scalp stands out white along her part. The mother doesn't answer my question.

"When did he spit at you?"

"Last night," she says and then sighs with boredom or frustration. Or both.

"Did you wipe it off in front of him?"

"Yeah, it's automatic. I can't remember not to do it. It's disgusting."

"You know you can't react to it, not at all. You can't let him see you do that. You understand why, right?"

She nods and looks at my snow boots, a slight smile on half her face.

"Wipe his nose," I say. She takes a slow look at her sleeping child and removes the plug with her thumb and index finger, flicks it to the floor. She returns to the TV. The child moves a little, a thin circle of blood on the nostril where mucus pulled off skin. Clear fluid now drips.

"A tissue." I try to say it not as a question, but as a *come on now* get him a tissue. I hope my tone carries that. She doesn't leave the couch.

The child opens his eyes and I flinch. I want to close them to his wet antagonism. The girl gets up and leaves the room, walks with flat feet. She returns with a wad of toilet paper and hands it to me, watches as I wipe, instruct him to blow, blow again. I look at him carefully and sense a softening of his posture as he relaxes into the sling of my arm. He is thin like a sick bird, deflated. He pulls in his bottom lip, sucks in at the sides of it, makes fish lips. His lips are the funnel for his reservoir. He usually spits with his eyes closed. He knows when they are closed, his mother's face, his grandmother's face, my face, are closer to his—that we feel a certain security. We can look at his pale eyelashes and freckles. We can see him as beautiful and try to ferret the source of his anger. He goes for full surprise.

Today, though, his eyes are open when he does it. I've prepared myself, as much as possible, not to flinch or show disgust. I let the spit make its way down my cheek and don't react. I hold eye contact with him. He cannot stand it, cannot look another person in the face. He crosses his arms on his chest, pulls his chin down, making himself smaller. I just wait, count the minutes of a commercial break and then stand to hand him over. She takes him and props him up on the couch next to her, his body still in that defensive posture.

I can't concern myself with the *why* of his anger. I can only address the behavior.

"Goodbye," I tell her. "See you next week."

Outside the door I wipe my cheek with my coat sleeve, wipe

it again, and feel disgust and loathing for myself, for the girl and her son.

I wipe my cheek once more in the car while looking in the rearview mirror. I want to see if my makeup has smeared. The curtains move and I realize the girl is watching me. I start the car, the usual cold weather protestations occur, and then I'm down the driveway and heading toward Corbina's house again.

She won't be home. It's only 2:00 and her work at the arboretum isn't over until four in the winter. Her mailbox flag is now down. I pause to open it and collect her mail to bring it in for her.   I park in the driveway and admire the contrast of snow against the deep blue of her shutters and red of her front door. She chose historical, colonial colors. It suits her, and the house—simple lines, little ornamentation. There are dogwoods and birch trees in the front yard, a fire bush. In the warm months she fills the pathway with flowers—an organized bohemia, the only type of excess she allows.

She has a welcome mat.

My key won't slide into the lock. I try again but realize the key in my hand is the wrong shape. She changed the locks! I've had a key since she moved in, just like she keeps a key to the house where she grew up. I cup my hands to the glass next to the door. Her dogs are waiting for me, wagging their tails. They don't bark.

I walk to the backdoor and try the knob. The door opens. The dogs run up to me, demand attention and affection. I pull off my gloves and oblige.

I toss her mail on the table and sit down, open my bag to pull out my files to make some notes about the visit.

It's clear the mother isn't working with the treatment plan. The behavior is becoming more difficult to address…At this point, I don't know how to move forward.

It feels so easy to say, to just say I don't know. The truth is I don't care. Each visit, I wonder why I'm there and how I'm benefiting them. The mother knows my doubts, she reads them in me. I half-finish the notes and move on to my next file. I'm to visit the home of a rehabbed coke addict who lives with her family on conditional release. Forty-five, peeing in a cup with the bathroom door open, her family gathered at the kitchen table, waiting for the hot cup and testing strip. They wait to see if they can love her another week, another week until another test. The smug and withdrawn face of the woman, the addict, as the strip determines she hasn't used. She collects the strips, places them in Ziploc bags and staples them to her bedroom door. A door of clean pee between her and her parents, if they try to knock, try to know her again.

Behind me, I hear movement on the stairs from the second floor. I'm startled—the sock's owner is here? Does he live here? I didn't expect that, not at all. But maybe Corbina's vulnerability allows it. The feet drag a little, scuff each step on their way down. They have to belong to the man Corbina wants to hide from me. I don't have to go looking for his presence in the house. I see his hand on the banister and am surprised by its age. The hand belongs to a man much older than I imagined. I turn to face the hallway and smooth my winter layers and the thickness they add to my middle.

He speaks first, "Brigit, I'm Martin."

I stand up, unsure of what to say. He has long ears and sharp eyes; he is tall and confident. He looks to be at least ten years older than myself.

"You're staying with Corbina?"

"Yes, for a little while. What do you need?" he asks.

"I just wanted to stop by, bring in her mail. I have a key." I pull it out of my pocket and lamely show him.

He sucks his teeth and shakes his head.

"No. Corbina told me you'd probably be coming over more frequently." He looks at me, really looks, like he is trying to see Corbina in my face.

"When's the last time you brought in her mail? Weeks ago? Months?"

I put the key back into my pocket and start to clean up my files.

"It's clear I stopped here to bring in her mail and then makes some notes on my clients," I say to him.

"Don't you want to know who I am?"

"A boyfriend, I guess."

"I'm not a boyfriend." We look at each other and then I shoulder my pack and turn toward the door.

"Are you going to tell her I was here?"

His arms are crossed, but I see he is hiding a tremor in his hand. He doesn't answer. I pull my key back out and toss it onto the table. He walks over it, picks it up and slips it into his jeans. We stand there a moment longer, each silent.

I found myself here, in this room, with this man, because I wanted to catch her secret. I wanted to see her omission face-to-face, figure it out. Yes, I had my files out, yes I made some notes, prepared for my next visit, but I hadn't gotten around to the walk through. Now I just want to leave the house to its strange misery.

He says, "I wouldn't tell her you saw me, that you were here. I'm saying that for your own relationship with her, not for me. If you want to tell her you saw me, do it."

I understand. I don't want her to know. I don't want to confirm her suspicions.

"I won't tell her."

"Really?" he says and shakes his head.

"Was she going to tell me about you at some point?"

"I doubt it, no."

The man's hand tremor has increased. I turn again for the door, twist the knob. I shut the door behind me and walk around the house to the driveway. I look up to her bedroom, where the curtains are shut. Martin stands in the doorway and watches me leave. He waves.

Dogs know shoes. Dogs know that, when a human puts on shoes, the dog is going outside. The dog hopes, anyway. Yes, the dog hopes. Have you read a dog's eyebrows?

People anticipate the future using a pattern recognition system. It has worked well for us as a species. Maybe dogs learned it from us, or maybe we learned it from them. We have merged survival skills.

We all practice being psychics. We are all mind readers.

The good stories happen when the human puts on shoes to take a nap and the dog is waiting by the front door.

I've dropped the pattern.

I plan to stay at the arboretum. It is a good job and I have lost the restlessness of my early twenties. I want to stay there instead of always looking for more money or something better and not knowing what that something better would be. The salary is livable, the hours workable. And I've gotten an informal education in horticulture. The boss, a stern woman with a deep brown tan and squint lines around her eyes took a chance on me. I didn't have any experience. I'd worked road crew, worked in a bakery, in retail, at a shelter. She saw I was most interested in grafting and assigned me a mentor. It is a beautiful thing—to take one plant and join it with another. I've come up with striking fruit trees and ornamental bushes, as well as prize-winning tomatoes on my own time.

I was able to save enough to buy the house with a modest down payment. I thought about a house-warming party as I signed the loan and was handed the keys. It was a passing thought.

What a physical thing, keys. I felt like I should be given new ones, ones that had never been used by the previous owners. Even if the house had been used, been lived in, my keys to the house shouldn't have been. I didn't like the idea of their hands on the keys turning the lock and entering. I don't mean I thought the old family would use the keys while I lived there. I wanted an old house with new keys.

After I moved in I forgot about those initial feelings and used the key like it was mine and had never been someone else's. I forgot about the divorce that had forced them from the home.

Money is tight. The house stretches my budget, but I am content to live lean. It is tempting to ask Martin for the money he said he had. Money that could go toward groceries now that I was cooking for two. But, what money? How could he have money, how much could he have on him? Why would he have a bill fold tucked away?

I didn't want to normalize the relationship by asking for money. I wanted him to stay with me. I wanted to provide for him.

Once, he pushed some money into my palm.

"Buy yourself something."

I looked at the dollars and wondered what I needed.

He read my mind. "Not what you need, what you want. Something you wouldn't normally get yourself."

I held the money in my open palm, at a loss.

"Get a hat, one of those ones with a big brim, for the summer. Keep the sun out of your face."

I laughed. I had a hat, I didn't need another one. It had been wet so many times from sudden rain that it was misshapen. I had to pull it on hard and hope to stretch it back. It was fine, though.

I didn't insist on giving the money back to him. I bought heirloom seeds. I bought Italian cauliflower whose flowers looked like complex, theoretical physics diagrams: triangles within squares, within cones, repeated smaller and smaller. It was thrilling to pick without thought of expense. I wanted to eat that little cosmos with butter and some salt.

Corbina has been cooking a lot more and she already cooks a lot. She is nervous. I am nervous. I'm not ready for this to be over. The other day, I woke up and couldn't remember where I was or why I was sleeping in a bed without my wife. Everything unfamiliar. A gutless feeling, a bad omen. I am not ready for this to be over. I have not yet begun to understand it.

The other day Corbina came into the house crying. She pointed to the newspaper next to the bed and my heart shook, ready to be exposed.

"China!" she had said, and reading my relief, began to cry harder. I had never seen her show this much emotion and I didn't know what to say next. *What a wounded creature*, I thought.

I reached for her and she let me hold her head to my chest. She quieted down and left the room. What can I possibly hope to happen? An anonymous life in a house I can't leave with a woman who is not my wife, my daughter, my girlfriend.

My son's image in the memory of a photograph his mother shot, of him taking a bath in the kitchen sink in our first home.

He is holding a plastic rabbit and appears concerned. The window is open to a hot summer day behind him.

I kept a journal until it was clear my mother read it. Now I keep lists of the weather. I record temperatures and conditions. I want the account of days, of temperatures I struggled through or enjoyed. Maybe a larger picture will develop, too. A history of a cooling sun. A warming planet. A bizarre tornado in the neighborhood that flipped someone's pop-up camper upside down. A basement flooded from a hurricane. I want to see patterns in all the surprises.

I record the germination of seeds. It is not exciting, but necessary. I keep the books locked in a drawer, the key stuffed down into the center of the tomato pin cushion on my desk. I don't know if Martin has looked for the key to open the desk drawer. I feel he has. What a disappointment for him—that book. Hardly worth locking up. Am I embarrassed by this account of my adult life? The reduction of days into the placement of my latitude, on the solstices and measurements of light? There is so little there.

I want to know what she sees in plants. I watch as she uses her thumb nail to snip the seed pods off a basil plant. She holds the seeds out to me.

"You think that's fair to the plant? Frustrating it like? It tries all year to get to that point, to make those seeds and you make it start over for your own selfishness."

She points to the table: hot house tomatoes, farmer's market mozzarella, and basil from her window box.

"Okay, me too. My selfishness."

I splash the food with balsamic vinegar and a little salt, pepper.

"You feel bad for the plants?" she asks. "What about the duck you keep putting on the grocery list?"

"The death of the duck is different."

"Tell me."

"You tell me why you do that to the plant."

"So the plant doesn't think its life is over. It dies once the seeds are ready and I want it to stick around a little longer. Basil is pretty impossible, though, very finicky."

"The plant thinks? It has an awareness of death?"

"Of course. It knows it has to create seeds. It's perfect."

"And the death of the duck is perfect, too."

She rolls her eyes, but I know she is smiling too.

"I can use that little gun your mom brought. Catch one in flight over the house."

"I have no idea where she got that. I don't know if it's legal. Don't I need a permit?"

I don't answer. I imagine pointing the gun out of her bedroom window at a migrating flock. I imagine having the dogs fetch the duck I fell. I've never killed an animal in my life, not actively, anyway. I've been like most, had someone else do it. Maybe I should. I wouldn't have too many years to carry the guilt, if I felt guilt.

"You are thinking about doing it," she says and waves her hand to get my attention.

I nod.

After finding the clippings of his son and daughter, I decide to search out what else I can find. I now have his last name. It sounds strange and ordinary to say his first and last names together: Martin Thomley. He had a life and a name and a family before he walked into my house. I had never asked for a last name.

I put his full name + our town into a search engine on a library computer. It returned a match. One out of pages and pages of possibilities. It asked if I meant "Martin Tomley." The engine could help me out a bit more if that's the name I meant to type. It seemed hopeful and willing to please. No, I think, nope.

A postman. A retired postman. There is a notice from about six months ago from his retirement party. I try to imagine Martin seated at a table in front of a cake, balloons framing his head, the wind from a rotating fan making them move in lazy half-circles. He looks miserable but is trying to put on a good face. I can see how hungry he is for the door and then hear the sound it makes behind him.

His tanned forearms are now in the context of a lifetime of walking a route. He retired from his job and then stepped from everything.

It was too much to ask, of course, to think about what our interactions would have been like if I had kept walking past the drawer with those newspaper clippings. But I had to know, right? I wanted to know what he found important enough to tear from the paper and keep near his bed. It was a kind of jealously, almost. I wanted to know his mind in a different way.

And then, a tight sickness in my jaw muscles because of the clear, logical question: what does he know about me that I've hidden? I pull my lip into my mouth, bite down, leave a row of straight teeth marks.

I had to tell Corbina. How could I not tell her? How could I not ask about him, find out who he is and why he is staying there? He knew my name; Corbina must have talked about me. I knew the stories she must have told, those same few life markers and the seemingly small choices that formed our narrative about the way life works. The way we work.

She would tell him:

I read her diary. Yeah, of course I did. I talked to her about what she wrote. It wasn't some secret. I told her not to censor herself so much. I could only see a faint mark, like breath on glass, of my daughter. I wanted to be able to protect her and I couldn't if I couldn't see her.

Spelling bees. I forced her to compete. At the time, I didn't understand the terror she felt, even when she wet her pants once before going up to stage.

Small islands off the coast, the rows of pine trees and crusted sap.

The surprise I saw on her mouth when she visited and saw I had added one of her baby pictures to my fridge. Her mouth closed quickly as she stunted her reaction.

And a handful of other things, the variable ones, the ones she might have felt more strongly about one day and not the next. The others, though, those were the ones I knew impacted her development. I understood that, but not at the time. How could I at the time? I had my own stories. My mother with one breast and two husbands, the inherited darkness around the eyes—people asking in stairwells, in private concerned ways, if I was being abused, if those were black eyes, no, no amount of concealer covered them; how my mom wanted to be from cultures other than her own, wanted to be another person with another story, one she could attach to with some sort of nationalistic pride, based on an American perception of what it must be like to be from somewhere else. A passive bully, like me, like Corbina.

Corbina could not deny that I loved her. She wouldn't do that. I've watched her step from me, from the circle of my body to a space that holds only her. I doubt she writes anything down anymore. Her hands are unrecognizable.

I don't know her. She has brought someone into her home.

I pick up the phone and dial her number.

"Hello?" she says, her voice rising. She is surprised to hear from me outside of our usual patterns.

"Hi, just thought I'd call."

"You scared me. I thought something'd happened."

"No, I'm okay. I heard something about bees today, but now I don't remember what. It made me think about you."

"Thanks," she says, maybe a smirk in her voice.

"I'll let you get back to whatever you were doing. Call me soon."

"Sure. Okay, bye."

I pop the gum in my mouth, working at it, breaking it down.

I swallow it and start over with a new piece.

I wonder if Martin was watching her face as she talked to me, or if he was just listening from another room. I wonder if he panicked at all when he heard it was me on the line. I doubt it.

I understand the camps and I understand that we are positioned against each other.

"Aren't you curious?"

"Okay, what did you do? I hate that question."

"I was a mailman. I retired not too long ago. They had a party for me. I don't miss it, not most days."

Her face hasn't changed at all. No surprise, no interest. Did she already know? After a long pause, she says,

"Seems like a good job, being outside, walking."

"Yeah, but I liked the other stuff too. Like how you know something small about a lot of people. Birthdays or anniversaries—all those bright envelopes at once. Letters from the IRS. Kinds of magazines."

"I don't think I'd care about any of that."

She looks down into her lap in thought. I can't tell if she's really listening.

"You're a bit oblivious anyway."

"Hey," she says and looks up.

"No, sorry. Not being interested isn't something I understand. "

She laughs a little, in a stooped way that places my words under her. I am slapped by the rift of our years. I feel like I'm talking to my daughter. I don't want to feel that.

She steps in, saves it.

"Fine, okay. Being a mailman sounds cool."

I had to monitor Boy Scouts during one of their community service projects. They were working toward some badge and I was glad to have small hands to help plant annuals. I never truly enjoyed the flowers that died each year and required a fresh start indoors. That period of tending seemed wasteful. I liked the flowers that weathered the winter underground and returned each year, over and over again. I preferred seeds that rooted firmly in the soil, sent their energies down and stayed put.

The boys were to plant cold weather pansies around the access ramp at the front of the main building. They were not thrilled with the prospect of planting flowers, especially these brightly colored purples and pinks. Only four sleepy boys showed up. They looked younger than nine years old, but, then again, I didn't have any kids. I had never been around children. I handed each boy a hand trowel and a ruler and instructed them on how far apart to place the plants and how deep they should dig. The boys immediately started to whip each other with the rulers.

I sighed, clearly not a parent, not a teacher, not someone who wanted to do any enforcement of rules. I didn't think they needed someone to tell them to control these impulses and felt instinctively, that, once I was out of their sight, they would start on the task.

I walked to the maintenance shed and unlocked the heavy double doors. There was a ride-on mower, a weed-whacker, and a manual mower. Most days, I pushed the manual one, strained my arms and back to make the grass shorter and more civilized. I had asked the board to allow more of the grounds be covered by wildflowers or native plants or even to just let parts of it be reclaimed by whatever species took root. But, the arboretum was first and foremost a place designed to make a profit, a profit based on the containment of growth, of shaping it and mulching oblong beds of prettiness, so my request was denied. I didn't have anything I needed to do in the shed; I just wanted a quiet place that smelled familiar.

From my seated place I saw the boys bent over the ground, diligently measuring their holes and then placing the bright purple, pink, and yellow flowers. I had heard on the radio that people should avoid digging holes because they release carbon dioxide trapped in the ground. The radio person advocated only small holes, surrounded by newspaper to limit weeds. It's difficult to acknowledge that the boys' tiny hand trowels were adding to the bulk of gas in the choked atmosphere. It's depressing, especially since people who garden are often trying to connect with the ground. The act of digging is a sacrament. The boys tamped down the ground with their hands. I could tell by their postures that they were satisfied with their work.

In the shed there were a few pictures lined up on the old beams. They showed a boy and an older man standing together near an empty hay cart. There were a few variations of this pose, taken as a series with slight expression changes. It was amusing to see them together and watch the faces become less static. I asked the groundskeeper if he knew who they were, but he didn't.

They came with the shed is what he said. I imagined the farmland before it was sold.

A cat stalks a starling just outside the door, moving its thin orange body along the ground, legs bent at sharp angles. The bird pecks at the ground, but seems aware of the threat in a peripheral way. The cat stops, tenses. The bird flies away.

Martin likes to watch me work outside as I make the first preparations for spring. He watches from his chair next to the bedroom window. I see his face in the shadow of the curtain and interpret his expression by the position of his ears. I can tell when he is smiling. Those ears make me smile as I turn back to my beds. The soil here is the red clay of a sea basin. Shells and bodies, seaweed and bones. Everything is decomposing, tossing off electrons, trying to become stable. The air is filled with elements, like Helium—produced by radioactive elements losing radiation. I look around and every breath is upheaval.

I find my faith in the transition of elements. In the segmented body of a worm, the apple core, the wood pulp. That is my fear and trembling: the finding of a rounded and smooth moon snail shell on the beach; pick it up, happy to find one without holes—only to have my thumb pinched by a hermit crab that had made the shell its home. How perfect a home, vacated and then filled, vacated and then filled, until it could no longer be used. The creature that created it, that built it around its soft body, long gone.

The fruit is both bitter and sweet. There are seeds, many of them, and they push out of the fruit onto your face and down the front of your shirt. The fruit is warm from the sun and the activity taking place inside it. There is ripening and movement toward fermentation. The fruit wants to be eaten. Seeds move through bodies. It's a rough risk, a movement toward variation, toward mutation and survival.

Continue to eat the fruit. Finish it; discard any stem or cartilage-type material. Hold a few seeds in your palm from this tomato. It's a dark and bulbous type, Black Krim. The seams split and grown over, sections of growth compete with other sections. There is a riot of movement outward and a celebration of excess. These tomatoes were discarded for a century because the need for symmetry and neatness was so strong. Vines needed to be heavy with produce. People wanted to shake the fruit from the stems into their palms. They wanted short and controllable plants.

They didn't want these black tomatoes with six-foot-tall stems, with rivers of yellow flowers and fewer successful fruits. There was so much green growing to make so few tomatoes. When the heirlooms were introduced back into the soil, the bees found their nectar unfamiliar and wild. They rushed the flowers, found beauty in the tallness of the plants and the way they wanted to grow.

Why contain them in cages? To help them grow, to make them produce longer and to lift the fruits from the ground.

I never use cages, but I admire, in some way, those who do. No, not admire, envy. I envy those neat enough to cage the plants and organized enough to tame. My vines runs into each other, develop strange tendons with roots that reach down to the ground. Do the plants want us to limit them and cultivate them, to make them more successful? There is a case for and against this argument.

Those seeds in your palm—dry them on a sheet of wax paper. Put them in the window in the sun, away from the dog's snout and curiosity. Let the seeds harden and seal their life in against the wet rush to decompose. Make a neat package by folding the paper into an envelope. Label.

This is a way to worship.

I bite the sulfur tips of matches and chew. There have been times I've held a flame to my wrist. Who hasn't? Who hasn't imagined death by fire? Or by water, holding their breath in the tub, making a game of it. Being old, I don't need to play.

I am certain things are moving that way, fire or water, or some lame bodily exhalation.

How many times have I looked at the phone and wanted to call Corbina? How many times have I wanted to tell her I know about Martin? On Thursday I drove by her house again, again on the way to the spit-in-your-eye-child, and back, back with a damp cheek and a blurry eye. I slowed to almost a stop. I hoped to see him moving behind a curtain. I didn't see anything except cold ground and bare trees. The house was dark.

I ask for some time off from work. I stay in bed until 9:00 a.m., watch the news, get into the shower by noon. I wait for her to call. I want to tell her how good my impromptu week off has been and how I am working on my house renovations and how well and busy I have been. I can't remember if I had called her last or if she had called me. I don't know whose turn it is. I want her to call. I want the small thrill of her name on the caller-id. I want us to be removed from the "your turn" cycle we had fallen into years ago.

I pace the floors of my home, upset by the unfinished trim work in the hallways. It was a project I started last summer, but I got overwhelmed by my need for exactness and had to quit. Now, the unfinished trim, and my need for it to be done and done perfectly, is driving me crazy. I need to leave the house.

I find myself counting, like one of my clients. She only starts a task when the numbers on the clock add up to something even, no matter the circumstance. Starting her car, eating—each task must begin on an even number. 1:30 is 1+3 = 4, 4—an even number. 1:31 p.m., though, that's 5. She'd wait for a minute to go by before beginning. It's a ritual I'm supposed to help her break, but I haven't come up with way to do so. The numbers are there whether or not we acknowledge them. They mark us, minute by minute. The woman sees the odd minute as a time when all bets are off. She sees time as it is. Those even numbers, though, those are more interesting to me. She has created a system where risk stops, where she is suspended in a transparent untouchable force.

Corbina doesn't call.

The paper came every day at 5:30. I was up, having coffee and a piece of toast. Corbina, warm in bed. I would hear the thump and rise to fetch.

The first time I saw my son, I was surprised and angered. He intruded in this life I had sought out and crafted. Intruded by swimming the butterfly faster than anyone else. The picture in the paper: tight silver cap, goggled eyes, mouth open, shoulders propelling him up and out of the water.

I closed the paper, put it down, and piled it under the other sections.

The next day I dug it out.

I stared at his face, the water spraying around him, the tightness of his lungs evident by his coloring.

What a demented drive to win. My children are creatures I do not understand. Their young brains and ambitions.

Seeing my son, red-face and successful, brutalized me back to the family table. His eyes red-rimmed, hair wet, the chlorine smell absorbed so deeply into his fingers you could smell it across the table.

My daughter, dark haired, ironic glasses, snapping her fingers at him in a hostile way, upset at some unthinking thing he did. So different, so much a mirror of my parts. And now, that stupid surprised silence of my chair at the table.

And she was next. I found her in the paper a few weeks later, also being successful. Cheeks round like her mother's, hair behind her ears, confident.

Reading the paper now held a different intent. Section by section, scanning. Then I could start reading in my usual order, rotating chairs with the sun, feeling my circulation start to warm in my old legs.

Why did I fold the papers, use my thumb to sharpen the fold, and then tear neat boxes with their images of success? Did I ever see them in the paper before I left? I thought back to our refrigerator. Magnets and a few Sunday comics. Nothing of note. How absent I had been while there, how present now.

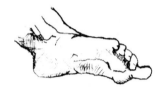

She had curls when she was born. The nurses combed them up into one large swirl on the crown of her head. The amount of hair an amusement, a rarity.

I never understood why she should love me. I never hurt her, no, but I spent her youth, her life, walking away. I walked the same routes through neighborhoods she didn't know. I memorized the number of steps to each house.

I knew which houses to rush by: the widower who kept the conversation lingering, his loneliness too much to acknowledge; the house with the pit bull—a giant mass of misdirected muscle, a baby with teeth; the one with the newspapers piled up in the yard—a bad feeling.

I was lucky to have such a route, a labyrinth.

Was she ashamed of me? A mailman?

Her friends with doctors for parents, parents driven toward professions. I could never tolerate people who wanted to be inside. I know she was ashamed of the dark tan of my forearms. I could watch it all in the way she looked at my uniform. She wanted to spend the night at friends' houses, never at ours.

Would she have cut me off when she got her first job?

My daughter always broke me. She knew that.

I saw how disappointed she was in her test scores. She wanted more. I wanted to tell her to relax, to be kinder to herself, but I didn't. I knew not to come between her and her goal.

She stuffed her pockets with pine cones, the sap on her face from her fingers, the joy I felt as my daughter exalted at discovering each small cone.

Martin makes me doubt myself in ways that have never occurred to me. I question my willingness to give. Is it a lack of male attention, lack of warmth, lack of self-esteem? Those cheap ideas that are accessible and indoctrinated. Yes, I missed having a father. I missed the idea of a father—not the particular man who made me. My mom and I were silent on the issue, but silent in different ways. I don't know if she loved him or if she missed him. She probably grieved being deprived the experience of raising a child with a partner, and not the particular person. In this way, we were alike. We missed the idea rather than the man.

I could just have it in me to give. It could have been there all along with no way to express itself, making another person breakfast, attending to their small preferences, providing company in the quiet space of the living room. I think this was part of the reason I permitted Martin to stay and did not feel guilty about his family, not much anyway. Sometimes I want to see pictures of him as a younger man. I imagine his family around him. Would Martin decide to make his way back to them?

I recall the second day he was here, the day I thought he had left when I went to the store. I had called his name, searched for him. He had smiled at me in such a stunned way as he stepped from the frame of the basement door. I had been relieved and quietly hurt as my voice returned back to me in the house: relieved of the burden of caring for him and hurt that he removed the burden. In the moment before he stepped from the dark doorway, I imagined him walking through snow drifts, his feet returning to red. But he hadn't left. He also hadn't answered me when I called.

Later that day, I walked down those steps and looked around. I couldn't find anything interesting. I lifted up the cushions of the old couch to see if he had hidden something there. Nothing but a few hairpins. I opened cabinet doors. He hadn't hidden anything of himself down there. There was nothing for him to find. I allowed so much unexplained behavior.

No, pushed it away, I think. I ignored it.

What was I hoping for, some kind of salvation? I was some beggar by the roadside, an old man in a field. I would have let the toes go, blackened. Dead. My fingers, too.

If I had been found, then hospitalized, an IV drip, those tan blankets wrapped around me in layers. Diagnostic tests, condescending doctors—no pity for the old man, no sympathy for a brain in decline.

If I was returned home, would I return to the side of the road, pick up my shoes and socks? Would I wear them again, like I had never made that choice? Could I look up toward Corbina's house?

I don't want those questions. I would not want my family's concern, their eyes waiting for my end; the veiled anticipation of freedom and loss.

The death of a parent is different for an adult than a young adult. The departed character becomes gilded.

The whole episode would have started distancing and distrust, suspicion.

What motive could have driven me from the house? Something less easy to acknowledge than an old brain. I imagine the phone call to my mother and brothers, the people I haven't talked to in years.

The numbers were written in an old red binder in a cabinet under the phone. My wife, announcing herself timidly to them, having met them only a few times at the very beginning of our relationship and never seeing them once we were married. They weren't invited to the wedding.

A family history of violence? Depression?

That family only called to tell me about deaths. I sent only unsigned cards, willing to be connected only anonymously. Even those cards felt like a compromise, a weakness I would regret. I see them balk at her questions. They tell her to leave them alone, the suggestion of a mental illness an insult.

My wife went along with cutting them off. She never challenged me. It was one of the things that made me feel closer to her. She said, "If you don't want them in your life, there must be a reason."

What reason was that?

It was easier.

What luck that Corbina looked out her front window. What stupid luck.

A first separation to prepare the family for the final one.

I wanted something to lift me up by the armpits and show me the world from that height. We all want to be lifted. To rise.

A cutting and editing of a person. A paring down. I wanted to pull in severely and be rid of all that is familiar and once thought of as necessary.

To die.

I start to hold my breath around him. He has picked up on the change, the slight shift in the air around me. I've stopped meeting his eyes. We can be complacent in this. I will not ask him to tell me his wife's name.

Every day I check the bedside table. I also open the paper and scan for missing squares. I haven't found any articles removed or tucked away.

The archetype of the fatherless daughter haunts me.

She must have found my newspaper clippings. That would explain the flux of attention and condescension. I imagine she is curious about them. She wanted to know and to leave it alone. Sexuality is something one can turn off, can decide to live without. Until someone scalds you in some way. I imagine knowing I had a wife was the reason she came up to me that afternoon. I had been napping. She woke me, the sun low around her shoulders. Nervous eyes.

We haven't talked about it and it's never happened again, not even in the slightest glance or look of knowing.

Something pulled away her guardedness. She unbuttoned her men's shirt with rough, stained fingers. The gestures of her wrists, movements I loved, rose to my awareness. Her wrist's movements in a hurried ponytail or while deboning a bird with grace and a sharp knife.

"You don't have to," I say and turn away from her straight hips.

She stands before me in cotton underwear. I am surprised by the girlish green and blue stripes. I half expected her to wear boxers.

She takes my face and turns it toward her body. She bends her right arm behind her back, reaches up and unclasps her bra.

She takes my hands and puts them on her waist.

I allow it, feeling shame, looking away from her. I pull her close to me to avoid eye contact and put on my head on her stomach. This is the first true contact we've had.

She slides her underwear down and stands apart from me.

"I can't," I say.

"Yes, I want you to."

"No, I can't."

She stands there a moment longer, shoulders loose, body quiet.

We are both embarrassed, not by the want, but by the momentary stepping out of ourselves. The step she took toward me.

I fold my hands in my lap.

She picks up her clothing and leaves the room.

I breathe out.

Maybe twenty minutes later, at the dinner table, everything is as it was.

Her shoulders are a little higher, a little tighter, but all the movements—the same Corbina.

"Your mom hasn't called," I say.

"It's her turn."

"Maybe something is wrong."

"Like what?" She looks at me a little more directly than I'm used to, then she looks back to her frying pan. She is searing thick slices of ham to go with the borscht. Pork is a rare purchase.

The soup is already on the table, a serving spoon in the sour cream.

She plates the pork and places it in front of me.

"Go ahead," she says, "eat."

We fall, bottles in hand, to the floor. It is a moment of surrender. The dogs leap to kiss our faces, to join in the celebration. They know inebriation and they know laughter. They are taken by its contagion.

Martin has one bottle of wine, I have another. We work at finishing them, not limiting ourselves, not exactly racing, but wanting to get into another head space. We needed to release ourselves from the space we've created within the narrow limits of our routines.

I never want to be denied this escape. Before Martin arrived, I drank beer. The bottles were lined up and then recycled. There were nights I slept in front of the fire—a dangerous thing, maybe. Or I drank whiskey for a sharper drunk, a clearer one.

Tonight we are winos. We grasp our bottles by the neck and slug.

I tell him a story about a man with freckles. I laugh about it, my stomach muscles controlling the air in my lungs. The air is pushed out and barely let back in.

Martin asked me to join him. He needed a night like this. He wanted to wake up and feel regret and this excess was the fastest way there. We all regret the headaches and dry heaving of a hangover. Each cell feels the forced dehydration.

"Why regret, why do you want to feel regret?" I ask. Blue jumps over and demands my lap. I allow him and move my bottle from the arch of his whipping tail.

"To make it real," he says. He laughs and moves to cover his stomach. He rubs his jaw; it's sore from all the smiling. He quiets and so do I.

To make it real. To drive it out. To allow himself to grieve the loss of his family. I haven't told him I know about them. It's so close to being spoken. I want to tell him *I understand*. But how could I understand, really? I do not slip up. I do not let him know I discovered what he left when he joined me. I allow a creeping gratitude to muscle out the apprehension I feel about not being able to keep this secret. I rest my head on his concave stomach and curl into him like a dog. He reclines against the wall for support and takes his large hand, large fingers, and runs them through my hair. They snag and pull, but he keeps at it until he can make clean passes.

The dogs have taken to sleeping with him. I don't mind. I'm able to stretch out across the empty bed. I can pull the blankets without the hard tug necessary to move a dog. Martin lets them out when he gets up. I've been tempted to climb into his bed and pull the covers up while he is downstairs reading the paper. I want this warmth.

But I don't. I don't want to get caught.

We have handled his appearance in my life by presuming its normalcy. There is nothing to recoup or explain to each other.

Over the months, I've stopped worrying about someone seeing him through a window or on the rare occasion he has joined me outside to smoke a pipe with his feet propped up near the fire pit.

Claire, my wife, my radish. You are owed a letter. I've started one several times. Each ripped into strips. I know you haven't looked for me, that the children haven't looked for me. I know you don't look at my coffee mug with grief. Which isn't to say there isn't love.

It is possible to be put together and then taken apart.

I'm not coming back, Claire, I'm not coming back.

I never expected to want the ground, the dirt. I had too much of it by eight years old after raking the yard, day after day that summer, to rid the yard of rocks. Mom wanted the grass to grow in full instead of in patches. I raked until my palms were sore, red; the dry rough wood of the handle left its imprint with a blister on the fat of my thumb. After I raked the rocks from the dirt, I dropped each stone into a plastic bucket, one at a time and listened to it clack against the others. I dragged the bucketfuls behind the shed.

The yard was that rocky. It was used-up farmland with no topsoil. I never protested; I just got it done. No other children I knew did yard work and there I was, building a stone mountain behind the shed. I raked and picked, dragged and dumped, and then I seeded the yard.

The grass grew that year. The nail of my pointer finger was permanently damaged and grew in crooked from then on because of all the weeding. Yes, weeding, too. My finger dragged the ground, the patio stone, and the mulched beds. Mom needed to prove something to herself, about her worthiness to own a house, a nice house that needed a nice yard. I was the tool to get that done. My job was to make the yard a green plot instead of a sand pit. That summer turned me off from anything to do with gardening

After a few years of living by myself I decided to try vegetables, something practical. No flowers, no. I didn't want that work—other than sunflowers and a few coneflowers—but they do the work themselves. I bought peat pods and boiled water, poured it over the peat and watched them rise to become spongy. I planted seeds. They became something. The first summer I had tomatoes and eggplants. The garden got bigger each year. I had sunflowers by the front fence to catch the morning. Squirrels came and stole whole heads. They bit them from the stalks and ran to a shaded spot to eat. They trailed seeds and petals, the huge heads obstructing their view.

I enjoy the old science, like the tricks learned over centuries of cultivation. Like planting carrots next to cabbages because carrot flies can't tolerate the cabbage's smell and leave the greens alone. I learned to drench the roots and avoid the leaves. The first year I felt terrible about thinning the seedlings. I tried to transplant them, too. Most didn't make it after the stress of being uprooted. I still ended up with thirty plants. That's the year I joined the farmer's market community. I mean, I stood in front of my little table and waved hello. The following year I did a little better; I made some safe conversation about harvests.

The first day at that table, with my tomatoes in little green crates—too many for me to can, cook, eat—I thought about my mom. I wondered if she thought it was normal to have me do physical labor (and the sun poisoning and headaches that went along with it) as an eight year old. I tried to talk to her about it once, but that summer was so far removed from her memory that she had trouble understanding what I meant. She had no memory of the intensity of my work.

I know Corbina will be at the farmer's market selling bare-root saplings. I learned from her that trees don't need dirt in the winter. They just need some sawdust and a moist covering. She won't be home and I want to see that man again.

I was out the door the moment the decision was made. I pulled down the driveway, turned onto the road, and drove too quickly. I didn't stop at stop signs—not fully anyway—and was at her house. I put the car in park and turned off the engine.

She had bought a stone rabbit and placed it in the garden bed closest to the front door. This surprised me; I would have thought she found it tacky.

I try the knob—the door is open. I step into the warmth of the house. There is a fire in the hearth. The house is calm. The dogs greet me lazily. Their coats are warm from sleeping near the fire. The man sits in the armchair with a book on his lap. His eyes are closed. I don't say anything. I wait for him to look up. He does after a moment, after some awareness of me, or of the shifting dogs, wakes him up.

"Brigit," he says. "Where is Corbina? Is she okay?" He rubs his fingers into his eyes, then rubs his forehead with his palms.

I feel my own age when I look at him. I sit down in the armchair opposite his and loosen my scarf. I pile my gloves and hat next to me.

"I imagine she's fine. She's at the market, right?"

He nods the same hesitant nod I've seen the children I work with do when they are trying to anticipate what I'll do next.

"If Corbina wanted you to know about me, she would have told you." He seems to be regaining some strength as he wakes up and, as he does, he gains menace. Instead of frightening me, though, it just cements me to my purpose. I'm best when opposed.

"I'm staying until she comes home. I want to talk about this. All three of us, talk."

Neither one of us moves. One of the dogs shifts to warm another part of his body.

"I asked you to leave us alone," he says. The dogs now hear the change in Martin's voice and they turn their ears in our direction. They seem attuned to the building tension.

"Let's just wait until she gets here to talk. I want to hear it from her." I look into the fire and feel his eyes on me. He is silent.

We sit together like an old couple with nothing to say to each other.

"You're probably the age of her father," I say.

"Why doesn't she doesn't know anything about him? Every child wants to know about their father."

"I'm her mother; I know what she wants."

"You still hold it all in, even though she's not a child. You punish her."

"It's my decision," I say after a while. "What do you know—

who are you?"

Martin doesn't answer. He picks up his book again and reads. He is obviously the one in control here. I knot the tassel on the pillowcase I'm holding to my chest. I put another log on the fire and use the poker to push it into the hot embers. It catches slowly, cracking and popping with moisture. It smokes a white plume. The dogs jump away from the hearth, startled by the loud pops and the tiny embers the wood spits.

"Oh," he says and raises his hand to his face. He rubs his temple and then rubs his hands together. He squeezes the fingers on his right hand.

"Oh," he says again and the muscles on the right side of his face drop a little as if something had pulled them down and held them. His hand drops, his shoulder.

"Martin?" I say and stand. "Martin?"

He doesn't answer or move. The dogs whine and lick him and then snarl at each other, confused.

I stare for a moment. I want to leave, but dial 9-1-1 and place the phone on his lap. The operator answers and starts asking questions. The dogs bark at her small voice. I hear her say she is sending an ambulance. I pace and watch his face. There is no movement in it whatsoever.

"Corbina, come home," I say out loud.

The police and ambulance arrive quickly. I grab the dogs by their collars and shut them into the bathroom.

Martin is still immobile. I open the front door and step back from it. I expect they will just come in and get to work. Instead, they knock on the open door.

"In here," I yell as I pull on my jacket. They open the door all the way and follow my voice. I leave through the back door and run around the house to my car. Corbina has just gotten home.

She parks on the street because the ambulance blocks the driveway. She slams her car door shut and yells.

"What did you do to him? Where is Martin?"

"He had a stroke. The medics are in there with him."

"You're leaving?"

"I was the one who called 9-1-1! I waited until they got here."

She blows air through her lips in exasperation and cuts her eyes at me. She leaves me standing there.

The EMTs have strapped him into a gurney and placed an oxygen mask over his mouth. His eyes are closed.

"Is this your father?" a young man asks.

"No, no he's not," she answers.

"Family?"

"No," she says again.

The man looks at her.

"He's had a stroke. Has he had others?"

"I don't know; I'm not sure."

The two men start to push him through the door to the ambulance. "What's his name? Are you riding with him?"

She shakes her head no. She looks at my face and then at Martin's.

"Just go, get in " I tell her.

"No, I'm not. I'm not riding with him."

Corbina leaves, rushes inside the house and then returns with an old envelope from the electric company. She uses her palm as a table, writes *Martin Thomley* on the envelope and then pushes the paper into the paramedic's hand.

The lights and the sirens are going and then they fade. Corbina looks back to the open front door.

"The dogs!" her voice cracks.

"They're okay. They're in the house. I shut them in the bathroom."

Her relief is instant and visible. We walk together inside and shut the door. Corbina opens the bathroom and the dogs push out. They rush to Martin's chair, circle it and then pant and whine. We watch them in silence.

"They know," is all she says before sitting at the kitchen table. I put water on for tea. She stares at the placemat in front of her.

"What were you doing here?" she asks, still looking down.

"I came to see you."

Corbina shakes her head.

"Leave, Mom. Now." She stands but doesn't look at me.

"I'm sorry," I tell her and reach for her. She pushes my hand away.

"No," she says.

"I just wanted to know—"

"What did you want to know?" I feel the history of our patterns. I hesitate too long and she pushes me. I stumble backward.

"Get out," she says.

She pushes me again, pushes me through the door. I step out into the cold and the door closes behind me.

What if I had never seen Corbina? Would I have sat, proudly, at my son's graduation from college? Would I have celebrated my daughter's first win in the courtroom? Would I have woken every morning to the thin and muscular shoulder of my wife in her peach nightshirt, her white hair on the pillow?

Yes, and yes, and yes.

I would have. I would have finished that life among those who knew me as Dad, as husband.

We're not dating, though. We live together. Or, I live here and so does she. The dogs are the only ones truly living together.

I've stopped looking for Corbina in her objects. I have understood some of her through them, but not enough.

In the books on her shelf I have found something of my younger self. I held the pages open to him and remembered his reactions.

My first wife on a beach in Devon. A serious summer. An elopement. The last bit of college. I left her on that beach, stepped away from her the way I stepped from Claire. The first marriage annulled, my family pleased to have me back alone.

Old family, old roots. A plot with our names on it in a forest and the foundation of a one-room house.

Maybe I was drawn to Corbina because she is without family. Her family a presence best thought of as a collection of shells on a windowsill. Things that once held life now bleached and empty.

You cannot tell anything about a woman by her underwear.

No letters. A few photographs without captions or years or names on the back.

Corbina and a red-haired woman on a beach, in one-pieces and with towels around their waists.

Corbina with a blond man, freckles over both their noses. They stand in front of an old growth forest.

Corbina as a young girl in a white dress, arms crossed in front of her chest, a deep, deep frown on her face.

I told you I stopped categorizing.

I am with Corbina because everything about her was a secret. She held everything close—everything that meant anything.

And yet, I knew she would help me when I was lost in the snow. I knew she would take me into her house. It was a safe gamble into a comfortable life.

I was only vaguely threatened by her mother and her mother's need to push herself into her daughter's life. A life purposefully closed to her. This interaction kept them going with its set of rules and expectations—the hurt and the thinking it would change, that some softness would come.

It was not hard to keep her mother's visit from her. It seemed a natural thing—forcing the mother to keep a secret, and keeping a secret from Corbina.

I napped and woke and only got more tired. I welcomed it.

I wanted to be here, in this house with this woman. To have it happen without a history, to mean nothing except that a man died.

I wanted my children to step from me into themselves.

I wanted them to move, fatherless, into the future.

I imagine Martin in a hospital bed, surrounded by the family he left. I see his wife and children and their fury and helplessness. I see a gray Martin, his system in shut down. There are a series of beeps to signify a pulse. The family that hasn't seen him in months does not get closure, does not get final words.

And there are no final words for me. There will be no hospital visits or holding onto the plastic bed rail that corrals his thin body. I scan the newspaper and look for his name and the proof he is gone. I find it around a week after he was taken away. There is a small photo of him in his mailman uniform, taken some twenty years ago. He had dark wavy hair, and a cowlick in the front center of his hairline. He looks proud but distracted, too. The obituary lists a viewing.

The dogs still perk their ears at the sound of the house settling. They wait for Martin's sounds. I launder his sheets. I box his clothes and his slippers and move them to the attic. I donate the cans of sauerkraut he requested but never ate. How obedient I was. I open the book he was reading to the page where he left off. The words are final: "begin a new existence among strange faces and scenes." What a bizarre and infuriating bit of fortune to have a goodbye in another's words. I put it back on the shelf with the spine facing in.

I decide to follow the hearse from the funeral home to the gravesite. The paper didn't mention where he would be buried, just where the memorial service would be. I park outside the modest funeral home, find a spot in the furthest corner in the back lot. Mostly men march in to pay their respects. They walk like mailmen even out of uniform. They walk with focus and an endpoint. The daughter—I recognize her from the newspaper clipping in Martin's drawer—steps outside to smoke. I didn't think she'd smoke, but then again, why would I? She observes the parking lot. Her eyes are dark. Light reflects off her lips. She smokes with a practiced comfort and draws deeply into her lungs. Her exhalation is slight. She crushes the butt under a patent leather flat, leaves the butt on the ground, and returns inside.

What would they say about Martin? What happy remembrances could they recall for everyone without showing the pain of his sudden abandonment? How would they explain where he was for the last months of his life? I wonder what the hospital told them, if they disclosed my address.

I see my mom's car pull up and park on the street and I lean down into the doorframe. She is wearing black and carrying a small bouquet of red carnations, the quality you'd find in a grocery store. We haven't spoken since he was taken from the house. She enters the building with her head down in the wind. She could be an anonymous co-worker, just another face the family never had the occasion to meet. I had dressed in black slacks and a pressed button-down in case I felt compelled to see him a last time. I slouch back into the seat and my stomach growls. The wind buffets the car and whines through the window where the rubber seal has worked its way loose.

I can manage grief. But after grief, what? The guilt of moving on. And then? A bigger echo that fades; a few dark molecules among millions. I grieve a man I never knew. His family can say the same thing.

My engine is off and a shiver pulls at my shoulders. More people arrive, get out of their cars, go inside. Quick goodbyes. My mom still hasn't exited. I sit for two hours. I know the scene inside, the highly patterned carpet, almost as vulgar as a casino. I know the folding chairs and the flowers whose meanings have long since been forgotten, but whose presence is ubiquitous: white tulips signal heavenly love, while pink tulips mean affection. Daffodils are rebirth. My mother's carnations divine love. Lilies are purity. And now, birds of paradise signify something— something like dependence on insects in a foreign place to do the work, something like globalization. I would have brought sunflowers, probably grown in an Italian field and shipped here— getting what I want no matter the season. Sunflowers mean adoration. I didn't bring anything.

Finally, my mother leaves. Even from here I can tell she has been crying. The family follows not long after and then Martin is carried out in dark oak casket. Men from the funeral home load him into the hearse. I turn on the engine to follow them. My mom pulls away in the opposite direction. She blows her nose as she passes. I direct the heat to my feet first and then to both my hands and feet. I follow the procession from a distance of several car lengths. The small caravan with their four-ways on travels outside the town limits past the flat valley and into the mountains. The roads become smaller and it becomes harder to remain invisible. I turn off into the parking lot of a wood cabin tavern and decide to wait. I can't stand at the site with his family, anyway.

I remember teaching him to swim. His dark eyes daring me to drop him; he told me he could do it, to let him go. The lake water was cold, glacial.

And I did. I dropped my son into the lake's shallow bowl. His head submerged and then his raised arms. My panic was complete, coming from a source a long way from here, from the bed where he was conceived, from how long we had been trying to have him, each bored with the other's body's roles, but happy, too.

I reached to pull my son back to breath.

He was kicking, though, kicking his way up, furious I didn't trust his instincts.

He fought out of the water and up onto the shore, a dark mass of matter. A boy.

The insides of the tavern are dim and pleasant. I imagine regulars gathering here and try to imagine myself as part of familiar group. I pull out a stool and sit at the bar. The bartender comes over. She's a young woman in a thick sweater.

"You might want to sit over there by the radiator," she says and points. "The rest of the place is pretty cold." The tip of her nose is red.

"I'm not staying long, but thanks. Can I see your menu?"

She hands me a single sheet.

"Do you want something to drink?"

I look at the drafts and select a domestic. She pours it and places it on a coaster in front of me, wipes up a small spill of foam. The menu is strange mix of breakfast and dinner. Lots of fried potatoes.

"I'll just have a fried egg sandwich. On rye with American cheese."

She nods and then walks back to the griddle. I'm surprised to see her washing up and getting ready to cook. She must be the only person here.

I think about my mom and her carnations and how she was blowing her nose. I take a drink of the beer.

The woman serves the food with a little cup of extra butter. The toast is already slick with it.

"Thank you," I say.

"You part of that funeral party? It's not supposed to start for another forty-five minutes."

She knows I'm not just stopping in, only regulars stop in. My impression of the place was spot on.

"I'm heading up there later, to the site."

"You been up there before?"

"No." I haven't had a chance to take a bite of the sandwich.

"It's pretty—that historic one with a little iron fence. Some of the headstones are broken. He was an old guy, right?"

"Yes." I take a bite and taste the fat of the butter and cheese. I feel relief.

She wipes the bar down, out of habit not necessity.

I finish the food and order another sandwich. I can give myself this space. I take more time with this sandwich, eat less from hunger and more out of comfort. I've been waiting—at the funeral home for the service to start, during the service for the funeral to start, and now for his family to leave him. I place my money on the counter and wave thanks, then crunch onto the gravel of the parking lot.

I get into my car, turn the heat up high and let it hit me full in the face. The road twists around old trees that were allowed to stay rooted. The caravan is coming down the mountain as I go up. The family's limo follows the now empty hearse.

The cemetery is a few minutes more up the road. It is in front of a single room house that has fallen into its foundations. There are a few sandstone head markers with the names worn down. Others are covered in moss after they weren't righted.

Martin's headstone is bright, clean. I step toward it into the small wrought iron fence that surrounds the entire plot. The family has tamped down the dirt and laid an evergreen wreath near where his head lies. I crouch down next to the stone and balance my weight on the balls of my feet, but I don't stay crouched for long. I rise out of discomfort, but not a physical one. I'm used to crouching. I use the headstone for support as I stand, then turn away and walk toward the car. Martin chose to leave his family when he came to me. No, I'm not sure leave is the right word. He stepped away from them. A clean step—like with a tap shoe. And here he is in this history we never talked about.

I feel like a failure for not keeping him from this. My own people had no collective ground for our bodies. His family plot was frightening. It was the inevitable place for all of them. But, it was enviable for that certainty, too.

I head back down the mountain. The tavern's parking lot is half full. I pass the old trees and their mossy trunks and drive into the flatness of farms. I'm not ready to return to the house, but I have to because of the dogs. They drive the majority of my schedule and create routines for me—routines that made me happier than when my days had no structure. I left the radio on for them today because I knew I'd be home later than usual. They wait at the door, pushing their noses into the windows that frame it. The glass smears with their hot breath.

"Hello, Blue," I say. "Hello Wilson."

I let them out the back door and watch them from the frame. I rush them in, call them to dinner.

Feeding is over in a matter of minutes. I open a can of beer for myself and sit down at the table in my coat.

"Start the fire," I tell them, these children who'll never outgrow me. They wag. I get up and start toward the fireplace, select newspaper and kindling and then build a structure to burn. I had bragged to Martin I could start a fire with just one match.

March winds, winter still. A hawk riding currents. Bulbs in the ground, dormant fibers contracting with cold.

God wears a pinkie ring, she told me. She smiled the first unselfconscious smile I'd seen. It held a kind of jumping breath instead of her contained one.

We are the same selves over and over, the daily radiation of the living and the dead.

I stopped reading the paper. I stopped looking for evidence of my family and their lives without me. Corbina mentioned she was going to stop the service, but she never did.

I dreamed my old mail routes, waving at women in bath-robes.

I seemed to be losing something of the reason I came here. Corbina found me once, sitting in the open of the front porch. She pushed me inside like a mother hen, scolding, scratching at the tile floor with impotent feet.

I read about the service in the paper. I've been looking for it, scanning the obituaries with fear. I remember his name, his full name, from that envelope Corbina handed to the paramedic through the ambulance window. The moment repeats itself: her hand writing his name in blue letters on the back of an envelope, the window going down and then up.

His obituary answers the question of what happened when he reached the hospital. It ends the possibility of Corbina visiting him there or taking him back to live with her once he became well. I learn he was a mailman and had a wife and two children. I'll go to the service in hopes of seeing Corbina.

I buy red carnations at the grocery store. They remind me of World War II buttons, even though I know those are poppies. I remove the cheap plastic bag and hold them by their wet stems as I enter the funeral home.

I am surprised by the amount of people coming and going. I hover near the back, not really wanting to be seen. I wait for Corbina. When it comes time, when I can't avoid it any longer, I walk the line the same as the others and place the flowers near his casket. I do not look at his face or stop to kneel. I return to the back of the room and sit on a folding chair, my head down but angled toward the door.

The next morning I wake up in the armchair. The fire is in embers. The dogs left me sometime during the night to wander upstairs and tuck themselves under the comforter on my bed. I had shut the door to Martin's room after he was taken away. The dogs have stopped scratching at it. I then realize what woke me up is someone knocking on the door. I am instantly angry, certain it's my mom. I can't believe she would be so stubborn and insensitive.

I swing the door open, ready for a fight. Martin's daughter stands on the porch. She hides her surprise, but not well. I'm not what she expected.

"This is the house were my father was picked up," she says. Her eyes are lined with dark purple makeup, her lashes are long. She is pale and the colors are vibrant against her complexion.

The muscles in her neck tighten as she holds back tears.

"Come in," I say and step back from the door to give her space to enter. She exhales and comes in, startles at seeing the dogs.

"They don't bite," I tell her. "I can put them upstairs, though."

She nods. I take them by their collars and lead them up the stairs to shut them in my bedroom. I look down at her from the landing. She stands in the alcove near the kitchen, looking both defiant and scared.

"Do you want something to drink?"

She shakes her head no. I offer her a seat at the table, but she refuses that, too.

"Mom didn't want to come. She didn't need to meet you. Neither did my brother. I looked you up from the dispatch. Why didn't you say anything to the operator when you called?" She doesn't clear her voice when it gets thick. "Who are you?" she asks.

I don't know how to answer, especially in a way that wouldn't seem like I was withholding something. She seems younger than I imagined her to be. Martin had children late in life.

"It was my mom who called. I wasn't here when it happened. I pulled up as they were taking him away. I don't know anything about what was said on the call."

She watches me as I speak, waits for me to continue.

"I don't know what to tell you. I'm sorry about your dad."

She shifts her weight and looks past my shoulder.

"Do you know my name?"

I nod.

"My brother's?"

I nod again.

"Ugh!" She's frustrated the interaction isn't giving her what she needed. She cries freely. I think I should reach out to comfort her, but I am worried that will make her angrier.

"I'm sorry," I tell her again. I decide to try a brief shoulder squeeze. She pulls away.

"What was he doing here?"

"I don't know. He never told me."

She shakes her head again, shakes it to try to make sense of this.

"I don't understand it myself. He was lost in the field across from my house. I let him stay here."

"He was never lost," she says. She has calmed down for the moment and takes a deep breath. We don't have anything else to say. She sits herself down at the table and looks around at my house.

I reach for the glasses and fill one with ice and tap water and put it in front of her. I also place an open whiskey bottle and two empty glasses next to it. She takes the water and drinks. Her energy has left. I sit down across from her and remember her proud face from his newspaper clippings.

"Your dad kept your newspaper clippings. He tore them from the paper. I found them in a drawer."

"What newspaper clippings, what are you talking about?"

"From law school."

She looks into her hands.

"He had your brother's, too. His swim meets." She frowns. I realize this information makes things harder to process. I wanted to help, to show he still thought about her and cared about her life.

"I shouldn't have come," she says and stands. "I shouldn't have done this." She hurries down the hall and out the front door. I watch her from the table. She turns, pauses, says, "He came here to die."

I finally take off my jacket and boots, realizing I spent the night in them. I climb the stairs to the bedroom. The dogs are happy to see me. I pull the comforter over my head to shut out the light.

❧

In this tent of a body, I'm selfish. Yes, I've denied myself many things. Excess meat, electricity, consumption. Too much CO_2. I have kept my living close to my body. But in these few months I became a creeping doubt, an idea, a presence in another's home. My close living had nothing to do with the man who walked into my home. And then it did. The need to have a secret became stronger than the need to do right. Martin the secret rather than Martin the man. His daughter forced the man Martin into this home. I say his name to the dogs. They prick their ears.

I loved her dogs, especially as they napped with me in the sun. I had dogs as a child. In that big house, with the others, the brothers and sisters and aunts and uncles and grandparents. And parents.

We had two dogs, a pair of brothers, like Corbina's. One personality was stronger. These traits must develop in pairs, the one feeding off the other. Just like brothers.

My siblings stayed close to the family, and raised their own families, and got together over the holidays.

I never wanted that.

I moved to the next town over, a compromise. Then again, another town over from that one. A shuffle away from them.

I stopped calling my mother. After many years, she stopped calling me.

I found out, during a rare call from my brother, that she had written me out of her will.

It took a lot of praying on her part, to do that, he said. We told her she should have done it years ago.

I sleep the whole day. The dogs miss their walks and meals and whine in discomfort. I rise from bed only to finally let them out.

The next day, I let the stillness return to the house and to my routines. I do not take time off from work. I ready the gardens with layers of newspaper to warm and enrich the soil. I cover other areas with carpet remnants to prevent growth.

There is the belief that the soul looks like the body. I imagine a translucent Martin. It's easy to become paranoid when thinking about the dead.

I refuse to believe the world of the soul trumps the world of the body. I can climb the thick branches of the holly and amongst the sharp leaves pick cicada shells from the bark, watch a cat bird jump and bob its tail feathers—clicking, whining—turning its small eye to mine. Birds have filled their bones with air in order to fly. We have filled ours with rituals to keep us grounded.

I find myself thinking more and more about the ground as an incubator. It holds the seeds and their potential, waits the winter through until the planet turns on its axis to warmth.

We wrap bodies in cement boxes to keep the ground and its creatures out. A tight space of air and gas, a closed lid—an environment still warmed by the ground. I want to let the ground in.

A bitter woman across from me. A mother only in biology and a sense of divide. I don't have the patience to attempt to explain her daughter to her—but she is not even interested in that. She wants me to explain myself.

This woman does not contain her contempt for the familiar way I'm sitting in the armchair in her daughter's house. A flash of dog tooth.

A stunted relationship coming to a head. I will not protect the mother.

She settles in, takes off her coat. She is ready, too.

I am grateful for this, a fight about the position I walked into when I left my shoes by the drainage pipe.

In the end, the body becomes a circuit board. In my head the rough pop and crunch of light bulbs under feet.. The sounds grow louder inside my head. Something is happening now. It is all of it too much, and then it becomes nothing. A body, a man, a life. All of it nothing at all.

What a desperate show at the funeral home. I drive home, smashing my nose into tissues. I knew better than to call her and ask to go with me. I knew better than that. I knew she wouldn't answer her phone if I called. Martin's picture at the funeral home was of a much younger man. His life somehow involved my daughter and ended in her home.

The ride home is over before I realize it. There is a miserable, season's-past string of lights around my door and a weather-beaten wreath. I hunch my shoulders in anticipation of the cold and then fight my way inside. My cat rushes to greet me by pounding his head into my leg and meowing for food. I throw down my purse and open him a can of food. He purrs as he eats.

The TV is on. I forgot to turn it off before I left. I sit in front of it and watch the station it has been on all day. Corbina doesn't have a TV; we can't talk shows the way I do at work.

Earlier, seeing those men line up and walk down the aisle, with such purpose, affected me. It made me realize what I had denied her. The few kind moments between Corbina's father and

I, how he liked to hold my cheeks in his palms. I could never even give her that. I didn't give her a few memories to build her own version of the man. I thought it was better to leave his face a blank, his name a blank. I wanted her to be made only of me.

If she comes to me I am ready to be her mother.

I spend the afternoon simmering chicken bones, carrots, and celery to make stock. Then five minutes with a cast iron skillet, butter, bread and cheese. I add pasta to the stock, some thigh meat. Soup and grilled cheese—an easy pleasure.

After I finish eating and do the dishes I sit down at the table and look out through the window to the field. I pick up the phone and dial my mom's number. It rings twice.

"Hello?" she says with both fear and surprise.

"Just hello," I say.

"Okay."

I ask if she wants to come over for dinner.

She hesitates, "Yes, what time? Today?"

"Is five good? Yes, today, if you want."

We hang up. I look down into the phone and then replace it on the cradle. I spend the next few hours cleaning the house of dog hair and dirt. I chop potatoes to roast and then cover them with sea salt and olive oil. The house warms from the heat of the oven.

I shower and scrub my face with a wash cloth and use a nail brush on my hands. I braid my damp hair. The dogs are attentive; this is the most activity they've seen me do in weeks.

Mom arrives early carrying fudge. She looks tired. I reach out to hug her and she returns the gesture. I realize she is avoiding eye contact. The dynamic has changed. She is allowing me to be an adult, to judge her. I gesture toward the table and the places I've set.

"I've brought wine, too," she says and pulls a brown paper bag from her purse. I take the bottle and then search for an opener.

"I think it's a twist off," she offers. I look down at the neck, and yes, it's a twist off.

We break the seal. I take down the two wine glasses I bought at Martin's request. A pair of them. I fill them with the red wine then hand one to my mom. We clink glasses.

I serve the potatoes with a side of roasted chicken I warmed in the oven. We butter bread and eat. I have a loose plan of what I want to say. I want to do something to start our way toward a mutual apology.

"You don't have to," she says. "You don't have to tell me, either. I don't need to know." I allow her hand to rest near mine.

BLACK KRIM

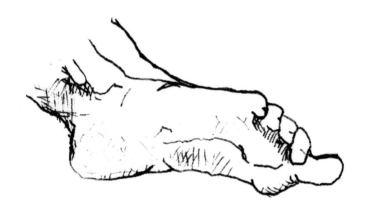

ABOUT THE AUTHOR

Kate Wyer lives and writes in the Baltimore area, attended Goucher College, where she received the Elizabeth Woodworth Reese Prize, and earned her MFA from University of Baltimore. She also won the Women Writing About Women contest sponsored by the Mid-Atlantic Arts Foundation and was awarded a fellowship to attend the Summer Literary Seminars in Lithuania.

Her work can be found in *The Collagist, PANK, Keyhole, Wigleaf, Exquisite Corpse*, and elsewhere.

In addition to her writing, Wyer is the manager of a non-profit within the public mental health system.

An excerpt of this manuscript, titled "Martin", appeared in *Unsaid 6*.

ACKNOWLEDGMENTS

Thank you to Andrew and Stacie and to all of Cobalt Press for your trust in this book.

Thanks to Katie Feild for her beautiful design, her friendship, encouragement, and enthusiasm.

Thank you to Gwenda Atkinson for early and much needed help with my manuscript.

To my readers: Ashlie Kaufman, Jenn White and Joe Young, thank you.

Thanks to David McLendon for publishing an excerpt, titled Martin, in *Unsaid 6*.

The quote on page 160 is from *Jane Eyre*.

I'm grateful for my cohort's advice and the discussions at the Summer Literary Seminars in Lithuania.

I'm incredibly grateful to The Office of Letters and Light for the huge kick in the pants.

To my teachers: Robert Evans, Madison Smartt Bell, Kendra Kopelke, and Steve Mantale, thank you.

To Joan McGill: ruby-throated, great blue, mummichog, Swainson's, black krim, pileated, harry lauder, sika, heartwood, lady slippers, cherry, green zebra, peepers, black crowned night, knobbed whelk.

To the late George McGill: I met a gin soaked barroom queen in Memphis. She quoted Shelley.

To my husband, Clint Wyer: I wouldn't have written this book, or much of anything, without your love and support. I'm endlessly grateful.

MORE COBALT PRESS TITLES

Four Fathers: short fiction and poetry ($15.00)
Dave Housley, BL Pawelek, Ben Tanzer
and Tom Williams

How We Bury Our Dead: poetry ($14.00)
Jonathan Travelstead
Due February 2015

A Horse Made of Fire: poetry ($14.00)
Heather Bell
Due August 2015

For more information about Cobalt Press publications, including our quarterly and annual literary journals, visit www.cobaltreview.com.